D1738074

Boystown 9

Lucky Days

Marshall Thornton

Chicago
2017

Published by Kenmore Books
Edited by Joan Martinelli
Cover design by Marshall Thornton
Image by 123rf stock

ISBN-13: 978-1542326438
ISBN-10: 1542326435

First Edition

I would like to thank my readers, editors, and memory checkers: Danielle Wolff, Joan Martinelli, Lemise Rory, Randy and Valerie Trumbull, Kevin E. Davis, Kayla Jameth, and Ellen Sue Feinberg.

Chapter One

It was a glum Monday in the middle of October and most of Chicago was in mourning. The Cubs had come within one game of going to the World Series. They'd gotten to the playoffs, had won the first two out of five, then flown down to San Diego to lose three in a row. Two weeks later the heartbreak was still palpable, on the El, on the radio, in taxicabs, on the local news, and in disappointed editorials in all the newspapers. The fact that we'd lost to a bunch of sunbaked, sushi-eating wimps—as Royko had christened the Padres—had not gone down well with Chicagoans.

I hadn't planned to go to my office that morning. Jimmy English's trial was set to begin the next day, and I was scheduled to spend the day downtown at the offices of Cooke, Babcock and Lackerby packing two cardboard file boxes with documents relevant to the first few witnesses the State's Attorney planned to put on the stand. At the last minute, though, I decided to swing by and check my messages.

I had a brand new Panasonic answering machine, which had features my old machine did not. For one thing, it had a plastic remote that you used to call your line and beep into the machine so you could collect your messages wherever you were. This eliminated the need to swing by my office and check my messages, except I kept leaving the damn thing in my desk drawer making the feature completely useless.

On the answering machine were three hang-ups, an offer to clean my carpets at a special discount, and a fumbling message from a guy named Vincent Renaldi. He'd been my main contact at an investment firm called Peterson-Palmer, where I'd done background checks for a couple of years. His timing was good. After the trial, I'd be losing the seven hundred dollar a week retainer I'd been collecting from Cooke, Babcock and Lackerby. I expected I'd be able to pick up other work from Owen Lovejoy, Esquire, but I didn't want to count on it. Another source of revenue would come in handy.

I was getting set to call Renaldi back when there was a knock at the door. Not many people knocked on my door. My office was on the second story of a two-story brick building on Clark Street. There was a copy place downstairs and a nondescript, unmarked door leading to the second floor, my office, the office of Madame Torneau—a hypnotist I tried to avoid—and the door to a CPA I didn't see often enough to avoid.

"Come in," I yelled, my voice still hoarse and cracking from an unfortunate neck injury I'd gotten almost two months before.

The door popped tentatively open and a tall, young man of around twenty-five stepped in. He was a light-skinned black man with soft brown hair that fell into tiny ringlets and arresting eyes the color of a sandy beach. He carried a bit of weight, but it didn't do him any harm in the looks department. A thin, beige windbreaker covered a red rayon shirt and a pair of black rayon slacks. He carried a paper bag in both hands.

"What can I do for you?"

"My name is Nello, Nello Mosby. Madame Torneau suggested you might..." He stopped like he'd run out of air.

"Might what?"

"I, uh, I went out Friday night. I don't know what happened. I had a blackout, I guess. I don't remember anything from around ten o'clock until the next morning. Madame Torneau tried to help me remember but she couldn't..."

"She hypnotized you?"

He nodded his head.

"Okay. Sounds like you drank too much and had a blackout. Those things happen." I thought mid-twenties a bit old to not understand what alcohol can do, but people make mistakes at their own speed.

He shook his head and opened up the bag. He pulled out a silky patterned shirt and a pair of dark blue slacks similar to the ones he wore. The shirt had a deep blue background and geometric shapes in red. There was also something dark, almost black smudged all over the shirt and the pants.

"This is blood. Is it yours?"

"No."

"Are you sure? You looked...all over? No cuts or scraps..."

"No, no cuts."

"Are you prone to nose bleeds?"

"Not since I was a little kid. And doesn't it seem like a lot a blood for a nosebleed?"

"Yeah, it does. Have you gone to the police?"

"No," he said. "I, if I hurt someone..."

"If you hurt someone you'd like to get away with it?" I suggested, which might have been a little mean but there was a real possibility he was a murderer. I should at least bring the point up.

"No. I don't want to get away with anything. I mean, it might have been self-defense. If it wasn't...I'll turn myself in. I just want to know. First."

"I'm kind of busy. I have a client going to trial tomorrow. That has to be my priority."

"Madame Torneau said you might give me a discount?"

"Did she?"

"I have about two hundred saved. That's all I can afford."

It wasn't much. My daily rate had been rising. For Cooke, Babcock and Lackerby I was on a weekly retainer that broke down to seventeen fifty an hour plus expenses. I'd have to figure out what happened to him in a little less than twelve hours if I wanted to maintain my rate. I wasn't sure I could do that. It could easily turn into the kind of job where I end up making less than a counter person at Mickey D's.

"Why not just forget it? Chalk it up to experience?" I asked.

"I don't know if I can live with not knowing. What if I did kill someone? There's a lot of blood." There was a lot of blood on his clothes, but there could be a lot more still inside of whoever had done the bleeding. Of course, it was also true that a lot more could have ended up on the floor, the walls, and the ceiling wherever this mystery person sprung a leak.

"Like I said, I have a client who's going to trial. I'm not sure I have much time to spend on this."

"Whatever you can do. I'd appreciate."

"Why not go to someone else? I mean, just being down the hall from your hypnotist, that's not a great reason to choose an investigator."

"Madame Torneau said—the last thing I remember about Friday was being at Jay-Jay's with a friend of mine."

"Jay-Jay's?"

He gave me a quizzical look. "It's a dance club on Halsted. Near Barry. Just down the street from here, actually."

"What kind of place is Jay-Jay's?"

Nello got even more uncomfortable and asked, "Did Madame Torneau make a mistake?"

So, that was it. That was why she thought I might give him a discount. Jay-Jay's was a *gay* dance club. A *black*, gay dance club—that was why I didn't know it. I took out a yellow pad and started taking notes.

"Sit down."

I only had one guest chair. It was chrome and vinyl and looked like it might last a few more days before it was time to put it in the alley.

"This friend, what's his name?" I asked, after he sat down.

"Evan Parker. He says we had a fight and he left me at the club."

"I'll need to talk to him. You don't remember the fight?"

"No."

"How many drinks had you had?"

"Two, maybe three?" He sounded like he was asking me, as though I might know.

"Have you ever blacked out before?"

He shook his head.

"How much do you normally drink?"

"I, uh, don't normally drink."

"Why were you drinking Friday night?"

"I broke up with this guy. It was my idea but I was still kind of upset."

"How did he take it?"

"Not well."

I slid the pad to the edge of the desk. "I need you to write down his name, address, phone number and any other information you have. Do the same with Evan Parker and anyone else you remember seeing that night."

"Oh, I don't know…"

"I can't find out what happened without talking to people."

Slowly, he began to write down the information I'd asked for. "I think you should leave Ty alone, though."

"Is Ty the guy you broke up with? The one who didn't take it well?"

He nodded.

"Why did you break up with him?"

"Because I love him."

Joseph Biernecki and I had encountered a few snags in our relationship that summer, but we'd hammered out our differences and fallen into the kind of sweet domesticity writers of Hallmark cards try to capture and always fail. Carolyn's Crew had gotten him a long-term temp job filing insurance forms for railway cars. Apparently, the cars were insured for each and every individual trip, so there was quite a lot of filing. He worked forty hours a week, every week. I tried to convince him he didn't need to, that I'd take care of us while he got ready to go back to school, but he was determined to work—which I suppose was admirable, though I found it annoying. I consoled myself with the fact that he'd stopped bringing up the idea of moving into his own place.

We went to work each day, watched TV at night, met up with friends on the weekends, Sundays I had dinner with Mrs. Harker—my sort of ex-mother-in-law—while Joseph sometimes went to see his family. Our night for each other was Thursdays, and our cheat-night was Fridays, though Joseph hated that I called it cheat-night.

"We're not lying to each other," he'd said. "It's not cheating if you're not lying."

I agreed with him but refused to stop teasing him with the term.

My old friend Ross had been living with us for most of the previous two months. He'd spent a couple of nights with his former boyfriend, Brian, during the week, but his sleeping there made Brian's new boyfriend, Franklin, anxious and petulant and nervous as a puppy left alone all day. Despite the chance to sleep in a real bed, Ross opted for my pullout and the generally less tense atmosphere.

Boring. We were boring and I loved it. Most people hate to think of themselves as boring. But they've probably never been beaten bloody in an empty building. After something like that happens boring becomes a lot more appealing. Luxurious even. For almost two months I'd reveled in my boredom.

When I got home that night, Joseph and Ross were playing gin rummy. *Born in the USA* was on the stereo. Springsteen's latest album was Joseph's new obsession. I liked it better than *Purple Rain*, but would have preferred a little relaxing jazz. I hadn't ever mentioned that because I'd wanted Joseph to feel at home, and now it seemed too late to complain.

"Where's Brian?" I asked. It wasn't a strange question. He was there most days when I got home. He worked a couple lunches a week at a restaurant down in the Loop. After his shift he'd stop by to see Ross.

"He went home early. He's upset about last night's debate," Ross said. Earlier in the month there had been some brief hope that Reagan might show himself to be the addled old man we all thought he was when he did poorly in the first debate. But apparently someone put vitamins in his Cheerios, because he did well in Sunday's debate. Even making a joke about his age.

"You're sounding better, Nick," Joseph said. "I'm going to miss the rasp in your voice."

"Don't worry, I'll just smoke more."

"Please don't. You smoke too much already."

I ignored that and lit a cigarette.

"Brian left this for you," Ross said, putting a postcard-sized piece of paper at the edge of the table. In the time he'd been with us, Ross had improved. He'd gained three pounds and could even walk over to the lake once or twice a week.

"What is it?" I asked.

"A voter registration card."

"I'm not sure I understand the point."

"So you can vote in the election. It's in two weeks. You need to register."

"What difference does it make? Politicians are all the same. They're all crooked."

"I don't think you can say that about Jimmy Carter," Joseph said. "He seemed like a really nice man."

"And look where that got him."

"Think about how much Carter did for Legionnaire's disease," Ross said. "And how much Reagan hasn't done for AIDS."

Back in the seventies, a bunch of conventioneers had come down with a mysterious illness at a hotel. A lot of them died and the government went ape shit trying to solve it. I wasn't sure, but it might have actually been

Gerald Ford who went apeshit. But it didn't matter; the real point was that Reagan wasn't doing anything about AIDS.

"Brian was lecturing again, wasn't he?"

"It's important to vote, Nick," Joseph said.

I didn't agree. I'd gotten closer to politicians than either of them. And politicians were a special kind of monster. Granted the ones I'd known were small time—state and local—but I had to assume the monsters just got worse the more territory they took in.

"Don't you think part of the reason Americans love Reagan so much is *because* he's done nothing about AIDS? He's letting fags die, which is what the voters want."

"We're Americans, too," Ross said.

Last I'd heard seventy-some percent of Americans didn't like us much no matter our citizenship. I was fighting a losing battle, though. I was going to have to fill out the card and vote despite how pointless I thought it was. I just wasn't going to do it right that minute.

"Gin," Joseph said, and put down all his cards.

I poured myself a scotch on the rocks. "Have you taken all your pills, Ross?"

We had a chart on the small, apartment-sized refrigerator for him. Given that he had a half a dozen opportunistic infections at one time, he had to take pills almost continuously. Including at least one that counteracted the side effects of the others.

"Yes, Daddy," he said, dealing the cards again.

"Don't call me Daddy unless you mean it."

"How do you know I don't mean it?"

"Because your clothes are on and your ass isn't in the air."

"If I felt better, I might take you up on that. Actually, if I felt better I'd try to steal your boyfriend. Consider yourself lucky." He winked at Joseph, who I was sure he had a little crush on.

I kissed Joseph on the head, saying, "I do consider myself lucky."

While they played cards, I sat on the couch reading the newspaper, sipping my scotch, smoking my cigarette. I'm kind of a newspaper junkie. At any given time there were two week's worth of papers by the front door. There had been a whole month stacked up but Joseph had the audacity to suggest I throw some away. I began keeping the extra few weeks at my office.

I quickly scanned through the Saturday, Sunday and Monday issues of the *Daily Herald* looking for some mention of violence near Jay-Jay's. I'd never been to Jay-Jay's, but I knew it was over on Halsted somewhere down around where Halsted and Clark ran into each other. I didn't find anything, which wasn't really a surprise.

I didn't know much more than Nello left Jay-Jay's at some point and someone else bled all over him. He might have left with someone who was gay bashed; those things often happened outside of bars. He could also have come across someone who was bashed. Either way, it wouldn't be in the paper. The *Daily Herald* didn't report fag bashing. As far as I knew, none of the Chicago papers did.

Joseph and I had hamburgers and frozen fries for dinner, while Ross took his six-thirty pills and had a bowl of soup. Ross ate six fries off my plate, which made me very happy. After dinner, we watched a made-for-TV movie with Sophia Loren and the guy from *Hill Street Blues*. Sophia plays a woman whose bastard son needs surgery so he doesn't go blind. To pay for the surgery she visits each of three men who may or may not be her son's father. We were all amazed that they got through the whole movie without ever using the word slut. Not that any of us had room to talk. We got a bigger kick out of the "Where's the Beef?" commercials than the movie.

About halfway through the movie, Ross got bored and called Brian. The rest of the movie was punctuated by his whispered comments to Brian. I imagined Franklin, lying next to him while Brian made cooing noises to Ross. I couldn't see how that was going down well.

After the movie, Joseph and I got into bed to read for a while. Joseph read *Interview With the Vampire*, while I read the true-crime book *Fatal Vision*. It didn't take me long to get bored with the Green Beret who murdered his family. I dumped the book onto the floor next to the bed, rolled over and slipped my arm around Joseph. I kissed the side of his face and tried to inhale him. It was fourteen or fifteen hours since his last shower and he smelled deliciously musty.

He moved my arm away and said, "Not now. I feel a little stomach-y."

"Okay," I said, moving away. I wasn't entirely sure I believed him. For a second, I worried he didn't want to have sex with me. Maybe he didn't want me as much as he used to. Maybe he didn't want me at all.

"Just go to sleep, Nick," he said, as though he'd been listening to my thoughts.

Chapter Two

Tuesday morning I woke up alone in bed. I hoped Joseph was making us breakfast, but I didn't smell bacon, and when I walked into the bathroom for my morning pee, he lay in the cramped bathtub half asleep. The water barely covering him.

"Are you okay?"

"Stomach."

"Why are you in the bathtub?"

"It feels good."

"I'm gonna pee."

"Go ahead."

I peed. Stealing peeks at Joseph as I did. He looked unhappy more than sick. I wasn't too worried. I shook my dick, put it back into my boxers and asked if I could get him anything. "Run some more hot water and then a cup of tea."

I flushed, ran him a bit more hot water, swished it around to make the whole bath warmer, kissed him on the forehead—which was hot, but it could have been the bath—and went out into the living room. Stopping at the front door, I grabbed the day's paper and wondered what I might put together for breakfast. My specialty was cutting up bagels and shoving them into the toaster. Ross was already standing in front of the Pullman kitchen pulling staples out of the refrigerator.

"Do you want an egg with a hat?" he asked.

"I don't know what that is. Is there coffee?"

"It's boiling. An egg with a hat is an egg cooked in a piece of grilled bread."

"Sure. I'll have one," I sat down at the little table and covered it with the newspaper.

Ross began buttering a piece of bread. "Is Joseph okay?"

"Some kind of stomach thing. He wants a cup of tea."

"Does he need Pepto-Bismol?"

I got up again and went around to the bathroom door. "Do you need Pepto-Bismol?"

"Huh? Um, no."

I'd obviously woken him. "Do we need to let you sleep for a while?"

"Yes."

I went back around to the living room and sat down with my paper. "Cancel the tea. He's going to sleep for a while."

People were starving to death in Ethiopia. The Cubs' best pitcher won the Cy Young award, which I hoped would quiet the whining I still heard around the water cooler at Cooke, Babcock and Lackerby. There was a long article on how well Reagan did at the debate; of course, after the first debate simply remaining upright for the entire two hours was going to get him a lot of praise.

Ross put a cup of coffee and an egg with a hat in front of me. I looked at the egg and said, "This is a one-eyed Jack. That's what we called it in my family." I wasn't displeased. My favorite food group was grilled.

"People call it different things. I've heard egg on a raft, egg in a hole."

"How many people have you been cooking breakfast for?"

"I've cooked breakfast for my fair share," he said, with a self-satisfied smirk. "So…the Jimmy English trial starts today?"

"This afternoon. This morning is jury selection."

"I thought you weren't supposed to talk about your cases," Ross teased.

I held up the *Daily Herald*. Front page below the fold there was a story headlined: **Jimmy English Trial to Start**. "If it's in the newspaper I can talk about it."

"What else does the story say?"

"Giovanni Agnotti…known member of the Outfit…charged with conspiracy, extortion and murder…ASA Sanchez hopes to select a jury and cover opening arguments on the first day."

"Isn't that a lot for the first day?"

"Most trials take less than a day from beginning to end."

"But something like this?"

"Typically it's the defense who slows things down. Typically we wouldn't even be in court for another year or so."

"Why are they moving so quickly?"

I shrugged. "I assume it's Jimmy's age."

"What would happen if he died before there was a trial?"

"I don't know. I guess they could continue, but I don't see the point."

"So wouldn't he be better off stalling?"

Ross was right. Jimmy might be better off hoping he died before they got the opportunity to prosecute him. But then, maybe he was planning to live forever.

I'd scarfed down most of my egg when I realized I was going to have to take a shower, something that might be difficult with my boyfriend asleep in the bathtub.

"I'm going to run to the Y for a shower." I hadn't been there in ages, but I still had a membership. I considered working out before the shower but decided not to go overboard. My daily regimen of jogging by the lake had ended during my recent recovery and I wasn't ready to start punishing myself with a health regime.

"Enjoy your shower," Ross told me, and then gave me a thoroughly filthy wink.

Jimmy's trial was held in one of the larger courtrooms on the sixth floor of Cook County Courthouse. The room was lined in a light, polished stone, which might have matched the outside of the building if they managed to sandblast off the few decades of grime that clung to the building. There were four very large windows to the right as you walked in. The ceiling was made up of painted wooden beams with flat fluorescent lights in each of the boxes the beams formed. The jury sat opposite the windows in sixteen leather armchairs that swiveled but were bolted to the floor—they could see everything, but were denied the right to pick up their seat and throw it. An aisle separated the twelve jurors from the four alternates.

The judge's bench was raised and looked down at the rest of the room. Next to it was a witness box on one side, and a recorder's station on the other. Almost in the center of the room was a long table where the prosecution would sit while they presented their case; the defense would sit at another long table along the side of the room, looking straight at the jury. Mid-trial, when it was the defense's turn to present their case, we would change positions. There were flags hanging from tall poles behind the judge, and brass embellishments running around the room near the ceiling—my bet was they had something to do with justice and that no one ever really looked at them.

The spectators would be sitting in sixteen oak pews, eight rows deep, and one pew on each side of the courtroom with an aisle in the center. The first pew on each side was designated for the defense and the state's attorney. I wouldn't be sitting there, though. I would be sitting in one of four chairs that lined the wall behind the defense table.

When I arrived that morning Jimmy was already there, seated at the defense table but pushed back a few feet, resting his hands on his cane. He'd aged quite a bit in the few years I'd known him. I can't imagine the stress of a criminal investigation is good for the skin; his was pale and thin as plastic wrap. Standing near him were Nathan Babcock—fiftyish, tall, patrician, neatly groomed—and Owen Lovejoy, Esquire—shortish, stocky wearing an expensive suit and over-large tortoiseshell glasses. We'd been friends for a couple of years and I was fairly certain he was a better lawyer than Babcock. It was unlikely he'd ever be put in front of a jury, though, since he had a tendency to flutter his hands about, overemphasize his S's, and call other men 'darling.' Jurors who took against a defense attorney were likely to convict regardless of guilt or innocence.

I took my seat against the wall, placing the two boxes of documents I had at the ready on the seat next to me. On the other side of the boxes was a woman in her early sixties, Nathan Babcock's secretary. She, too, was there in case of emergency. She didn't bother to say hello to me, so I didn't bother to say hello to her.

Mrs. Barnes, as I later learned she was called, probably judged me as insignificant based on what I wore. I had on my old corduroy jacket. I'd had it dry-cleaned, but it still looked like it had been run over by a semi. Beneath the jacket I had on a white Oxford shirt, a plaid woolen tie, 501s and brown, Florsheim penny loafers. I should have upgraded my wardrobe. I certainly had enough money to, it's just that every time I went into Marshall Field's or Carson, Pirie, Scott all the clothes seemed designed for either East Coast bankers with a penchant for weekend golf or some costumer's idea of which pastel an undercover cop might wear in Miami.

At the State's table, Linda Sanchez stood with two other ASAs. She was raven-haired and dark-eyed. She wore a blue pin-striped suit over a cream-colored blouse that boasted a big floppy bow around her neck. On her feet, she wore a pair of Nikes, which she eventually traded for a pair of conservative, two-inch heels she carried in her briefcase. The two other ASAs were men. One was forty and doughy, and even from twenty feet away I could see he resented Sanchez, who was clearly in charge. The other ASA was Tony Stork.

Tony was around thirty, tall, lanky, with an upper crust North Shore look to him. He had sand-colored hair and dark eyes rimmed with thick lashes. I was surprised to see him on their team. A few years before, he'd prosecuted a guy named Campbell Wayne, who tried to throw me in front of a CTA train. He'd also given me a memorable blow job in an empty interview room. Since I'd also dallied with Owen Lovejoy, Esquire, that meant I'd had sex with lawyers on each side of the aisle. I decided it might not be good to spread that information around.

As it neared ten, the pews filled. A good number of the spectators seemed to be press, but there were also a few other people I recognized. Lydia Agnotti was there sitting in a pew near the back. She was Jimmy's granddaughter. We'd met when she'd tricked her brother into killing their stepfather. Her brother was now in prison, while she roamed the streets.

Sliding into the front pew were Beverly Harlington and Rose Hansen. Beverly was Lydia's mother, whose first husband was Jimmy's deceased son—Lydia didn't happen to have anything to do with his death. Rose was Jimmy's daughter. She and Beverly were more appropriately dressed for afternoon tea than court. On the other side of the room, looking somber and determined, was Deanna Hanson with her much older boyfriend, Turi Bova. I have to say, with all of Jimmy's family there it looked more like a custody case than a mob trial.

Aside from the press and the family, there were a couple of other middle-aged men who looked like they might be members of the Outfit: their dark polyester slacks, golf shirts, windbreakers and Italian shoes were dead giveaways. At the top of Jimmy's food chain was a man called Doves. My guess was that these guys would be bringing Doves the news of the day.

I didn't understand why Rose and Deanna were there. They were both going to be witnesses and I doubted they'd be testifying on the first day, so I wondered what made them think they'd be able to remain in the courtroom. When I was on the job I'd had to testify about a dozen times. Each time I'd had to wait in the hallway until I was called. I didn't know why Rose and Deanna thought they'd be entitled to watch the trial, other than the fact that they felt entitled in general.

A bailiff walked into the court from the back; a red-haired woman wearing a khaki and green uniform. In her late forties, she had very large breasts jutting out, making me wonder if she even knew there was a walkie-talkie and gun on her belt.

"Please rise."

We did.

"Cook County Criminal Court is now in session. The Honorable Judge Martin Corbin presiding."

Next came a meek looking court reporter in a brown dress with a white lace collar. Behind her, Judge Corbin in his black robes. He was in his late fifties, with thinning white hair and a puffy face. Once he got situated behind the bench he said, "Please be seated."

We sat.

The judge looked around and then said, "This is State of Illinois v. Giovanni Agnotti. Is that correct?"

ASA Sanchez and Nathan Babcock each stood and said, "Yes, your honor."

"I like to make sure. Cousin of mine went into the hospital to have a testicle removed. They took the wrong one. Now he has none. I wouldn't like to come to work in the morning and hear the wrong case."

It was a crazy thing to say. Most of the people in the room didn't know whether to laugh or not. Certainly, Jimmy's team was confused. The ASAs, though, they knew to laugh and were putting on a show of it. Judge Corbin looked pleased with the response he got. I wondered if he began every trial with this same joke.

"Before we begin jury selection, are there motions?"

ASA Sanchez stood up and motioned that witnesses be excluded from the courtroom. "With the exception of Mr. Agnotti's family members, of course."

Since Rose and Deanna were witnesses for the state's attorney, I fully expected Nathan Babcock to object and ask that they be excluded. Instead, he stayed seated and said, "No objections, your honor."

I was surprised by that, but from the look on her face not as much as ASA Sanchez. For a moment, I thought she might jump up and say, "Oh no, your honor, never mind."

The judge announced that jury selection was going to begin. The bailiff went to get the first round of sixteen jurors to be questioned. Owen looked over his shoulder then pushed his chair back to me.

"Have you spent much time in a courtroom?" he asked.

"A bit."

"We're not expecting this to go more than two weeks. Maybe less."

"What about Devlin? Will you be able to talk about him?" In my opinion, the best defense for Jimmy would be to focus on Devlin and his creative ways of gathering confessions. Beating the crap out of witnesses tends to make their testimony inadmissible.

"There was a motion to suppress two weeks ago. I guess we'd call it a draw. We can't bring him up, but it's impossible to keep him completely out since he interviewed most of their witnesses."

"So you won't be calling me?" Devlin was responsible for pretty much all of my recent injuries. I would have loved to testify about him.

"No," Owen said. "We can't put you on the stand or present testimony about Devlin's prosecution."

"Will they be calling him to testify?"

"No. The first question is always name and address. If he didn't say Cook County Jail he'd be perjuring himself and if he tells the court where he currently lives we get to ask why."

"So this is going to boil down to how much you can get in about Devlin without asking questions about Devlin."

He gave me a devilish smile. "Darling, you should have been a lawyer."

When the prospective jurors got settled, the judge told the attorneys they could begin. Sanchez and Babcock took turns asking bland questions like, "Do you think you can be impartial?" Occasionally, Sanchez would ask a juror how they felt about police officers. If she didn't like the answer she'd dismiss the juror. Babcock asked a similar question about the restaurant business and let go of a couple of jurors who'd once been waitresses. It was all pretty obvious stuff.

While I sat there, I wondered exactly what was going on. The most damning evidence against Jimmy would come from his granddaughter, Deanna. She'd been informing on him for more than a year, providing Operation Tea and Crumpets—the task force investigating Jimmy—with a journal that detailed Jimmy's activities for nearly thirty years. Keeping something like a journal was a stupid idea, but Jimmy admitted to me that he'd done just that. Then, when I finally got to look at a much-copied Xerox in discovery, I'd realized there was no way Jimmy had written the journal. The handwriting was wrong. So, he'd lied to me. What I hadn't figured out was, why?

The case began to crumble when it became obvious that Devlin was a bad cop. The Feds dropped it like a hot potato, but ASA Sanchez persisted. I had an inkling she thought the publicity could only be good for her career. What I didn't understand was the defense. Why hadn't they insisted the handwriting in the journal be compared to Deanna's? At this point, given the weakness of the prosecution's case, just suggesting that Deanna had written the journal herself might have been enough to get them to drop the charges.

Of course, Jimmy could simply be protecting Deanna. Providing false evidence was a crime, as was lying to federal agents. Conceivably, she could spend half a decade in prison. Was Jimmy counting on his expensive lawyers to get him off without exposing his granddaughter's lies? I'd known Jimmy for a while. That seemed like something he'd do. I knew family was important to him. His grandson was in prison; I doubted he wanted any more of his grandchildren to end up there.

Jury selection took a bit more than two hours. Once the jury was empanelled, Judge Corbin gave them a little speech.

"This is my courtroom. I make the rules here and what I say goes. You'll note that the state attorneys or the defense attorneys will often object to my decisions. In fact, they will likely try to influence you by the objections they make. Don't let them."

He stopped to give both sides in the case a dirty look.

"This is an important trial that has garnered interest from the local press. You are not to read any of the articles written about the trial or watch any news programs that include stories about the trial. If at any time I think any one of you has ignored these instructions I will sequester you all."

Now he gave the jurors a dirty look.

"There's something I want to make very clear to all twelve of you jurors and also the four alternates. At this moment in time, Giovanni Agnotti is innocent." I watched ASA Sanchez flinch when he said it. "He's innocent because in the American system we are all innocent until proven guilty. The fact that Ms. Sanchez believes she can prove that Mr. Agnotti is guilty does not make it so. He is innocent until the state proves to you he is not. And on that note, we should break for lunch. We will reconvene at two-thirty."

It wasn't quite one. We had nearly two hours before court began again. Not enough time to go back to the office, but enough time to get really bored. Rose and Beverly were already hovering around Jimmy—from the comments they made it seemed as though Jimmy's driver was going to drive them somewhere "decent" for lunch. Babcock seemed to be tagging along, though I wasn't sure I had an invitation. When the party began to walk out of the courtroom, I noticed Lydia Agnotti hovering nearby. She was pointedly ignored by her mother and her aunt; Jimmy may have nodded at her, but I couldn't be sure.

When they'd walked completely out of the courtroom, Lydia turned and glared at me. My exposing her as the one truly responsible for her stepfather's death had caused the estrangement with her family, so we weren't exactly friends.

I'm not sure, but she may have hissed at me.

Chapter Three

Owen begged off lunch, saying he had to cab it back to the office and return a few calls. I assumed his secretary would arrange something pleasant to eat at his desk. The area around the courtroom was notorious for its lack of decent restaurants. That hadn't quite sunk in from when I'd been there before, since I'd only come to testify and then gone home. I'd never sat through an entire trial nor dealt with the problem of lunch breaks.

I wandered around a bit and finally found a stand-up snack shop on the first floor, where I was able to have a bowl of chili that came with as many tiny bags of oyster crackers as I could stomach. I stood at a shelf that ran along the wall with a dozen, nervous, petty criminals. It wasn't that the lawyers and judges in the building looked much more honest, they just wore better clothes.

I pulled a small reporter's pad out of my side pocket and started to make some notes about the Mosby case. Given my involvement with Jimmy's trial, my approach to the case was going to have to be about picking off the low-hanging fruit. Whatever was easy and quick, I'd do first. Probably not the most organized way to approach an investigation, but Nello Mosby had agreed to take what he could get.

While slurping down the chili and chasing it with a root beer, I made a list of people I needed to interview. I'd brought the sheet Nello had written out for me, so I had some idea who I wanted to talk to. The most important were his friend Evan Parker and his former boyfriend Tyrone Carter. I'd asked him to write down the names of anyone else he remembered seeing that night and he had. He'd seen people named Smooth Willy, Jammin' Johnny, Maurice-Maurice and Jellyroll. Other than Jammin' Johnny, he didn't know any of these people well enough to have their phone numbers, addresses or, for that matter, legal names.

I was definitely going to have to make a stop at Jay-Jay's to talk to the bartender to see if he remembered and/or had heard anything. Since the referral had come from Madame Torneau, I put her down on my list of people to talk to. The fact that there hadn't been any news reports of violence in the area didn't mean it hadn't happened, so I added Frank Connors, Harker's old partner, to the list. He could check and see if anyone not worth mentioning in the newspaper happened to bleed to death near the dance club.

As I finished up the chili, which wasn't half bad, I sketched out some of the questions I needed to ask each of the people on my list. Then I went in search of a pay phone. It took a while, but I found a bank of four phones stuck to the wall next to the men's room. I pulled out Nello's sheet, unfolded it on the metal shelf that ran beneath the phones and dumped out some change next to it. There were only three phone numbers on the page: Evan Parker, Nello's boyfriend Ty, and another for Jammin' Johnny.

When I talked to Evan and Ty, I wanted to do it face to face. I also wanted to know a little more about what was really going on before I met them. I decided to start small and call Jammin' Johnny. I lit a cigarette and thought things through. I could call Jammin' Johnny and tell him who I was and what I wanted to know, but there was a strong possibility he wouldn't want to tell me. I balanced my cigarette on the metal shelf, plopped a quarter in the slot and dialed.

After six rings, a man answered. "Who is this?"

"Is this Jammin' Johnny?"

"Yeah. Who are you?"

"I'm investigating an incident that happened outside Jay-Jay's on Friday night."

"Don't know nothing about that."

"But you were at Jay-Jay's and you know something happened."

"Didn't say that."

"You know Nello Mosby, right?"

"I don't wanna talk to you."

"I can send out an officer." I couldn't, but he didn't know that.

"Nello tell you to ask me this shit? Did he?"

"Look, just tell me what happened outside Jay-Jay's on Friday and I'll leave you alone."

"Nothing happened outside Jay-Jay's." There was the tiniest inflection on the word outside.

"Something happened inside?"

"I don't know anything about anything."

"Except you do. Something happened inside Jay-Jay's and you know it."

"You tell Nello he's got a big mouth," he said, and then he hung up.

As I absorbed what I'd learned, I took the last drag of my cigarette. There was a trash can with a sand-filled ashtray on top right outside the men's room. I walked over and pressed my butt into the sand.

Nello had gotten covered in blood inside Jay-Jays. I went back to the pay phone and called Evan Parker. I got an answering machine and decided not to leave a message. I didn't bother with Ty, the boyfriend. Not yet. It was time to go back to the sixth floor.

When court reconvened, ASA Sanchez, stood up, smoothed her skirt, and told the judge her remarks would take about forty-five minutes. He nodded. She studied a pad in front of her and then walked over to stand in front of the jury.

"*Webster's New World Dictionary* defines the word conspiracy as 'an illegal act planned and committed by two or more persons.' By the time I finish presenting this case there will be no doubt in your minds that Giovanni Agnotti is guilty of planning and committing a host of illegal acts with his henchmen. In fact, there will be no doubt that Giovanni Agnotti sits atop a well-oiled criminal conspiracy that rivals the best corporations in the Loop in terms of efficiency and profitability. Come to think of it, that's how you should think of Giovanni Agnotti, as a criminal CEO."

She paused, took a few steps to her left, and then continued, "The Illinois Criminal Code section eight dash two defines a conspiracy as..."

And then she went on to quote several legal paragraphs. I thought it was interesting the way she'd introduced a simple idea, a word in layman's terms, and then brought in the more complicated legal definition. Of course, the jury would keep falling back on the broader, less legalistic dictionary definition. Giving Sanchez the greatest likelihood of a conviction.

Then, in extensive detail, she outlined the ways in which Jimmy was guilty of operating a criminal conspiracy. When she was finished, she followed the same pattern with extortion, covering both the dictionary and legal definitions. Carefully, she walked the jury through what she planned to demonstrate about Jimmy and extortion. Finally, she got to murder.

"We all know what a murderer is, a murderer is a person who causes another person to die. It doesn't matter whether that person fires a gun himself or whether he instructs someone else to do it. The important part is cause. In the case before you, the important question is did Giovanni Agnotti cause the murder of Shady and Josette Perrelli. And when I'm finished you will know that he did."

By this point she'd planted herself dead center in front of the jury.

"When I'm finished, you will have no doubt that Giovanni Agnotti conspired to commit extortion and murder."

The courtroom was dead silent. Sanchez calmly went back to the State's table and sat down. The doughy ASA looked to be whispering congratulations into her ear. Tony Stork glanced over at me and seemed to smile. I glanced down at my Swatch and noted that ASA Sanchez had taken ten minutes less than she'd expected.

I moved the watch around on my wrist. I wasn't crazy about it. The plastic band made my wrist sweat and it was entirely too trendy, but Joseph had given it to me for our six-month anniversary, so I had to wear it. My old, serviceable Timex lay in a drawer.

Nathan Babcock got up to take his stab at the jury. He didn't bother telling the judge how long he'd be. He simply walked over to the jury and gave them a charming, knowing smile. I swear there was a twinkle in his eye.

"It was very kind of ASA Sanchez to give you a vocabulary lesson, wasn't it? Unfortunately, what she doesn't have are facts. Don't worry, I won't insult you by explaining what a fact is."

There was a soft chuckle from the gallery. Sanchez struggled not to frown as he continued to discuss the dearth of facts she'd built her case on. The jury, though, hung on Babcock's every word. He had so much charisma he almost glowed. Watching him, I understood the way he worked with Owen. Yeah, Owen was too clearly gay to stand up in front of a jury, but it hadn't occurred to me that Babcock would be so damn good. No wonder Owen was content to be the puppet master.

Babcock went on for a few more minutes, outlining the facts the State did not have. They had no physical evidence of the murders, no eyewitnesses to the murders, and no motive for the murders. He leaned in toward the jury, as though they were already old friends, "One wonders why the State bothered to define the word for you."

As he strolled around the courtroom, the jury couldn't take their eyes off him. And no one else could either. Jimmy's daughter, daughter-in-law and both granddaughters watched his every move. And so did the Outfit guys.

Babcock outlined the problems the Chicago Police Department had had over the years staying within the law: the various FBI investigations, court decrees and, finally, their reputation for corruption, brutality and all out terribleness. By the time he was done I was ashamed of having ever been with the CPD. To finish off, Babcock briefly and convincingly painted a picture of Jimmy as a slightly addled old man who, after a lifetime in the restaurant supplies business, had simply failed to pay off the right people.

Once Babcock was back in his seat, the judge asked Sanchez, "Who's your first witness, Ms. Sanchez?" She frowned again, as she made a show of pulling out her witness list. I was fairly certain she hated being called anything but ASA Sanchez, and that she actually knew who her first witness was going to be.

"Our first witness is going to be Jonathon Lidell."

"And how long do you think his testimony will take?"

"Possibly an hour, you honor."

I glanced at my Swatch. It was four twenty-five. The scowl on Judge Corbin's face told me what was about to happen. "Why don't we put that off until tomorrow then. Court will reconvene at 10 a.m." He slammed down his gavel and then hurried out of the courtroom like he had an appointment he was late for.

The Cook County Courthouse is not in a convenient spot, not for good restaurants and not for good public transportation. Though there were many train tracks nearby there were no El lines. If I wanted to take public transportation I would have had to take a bus. Well, many buses. You'd think they'd have worked this out a bit better, given the number of Chicagoans who did regular business at the Courthouse. We had a bad reputation; the rest of America believed that Chicago was a violent, lawless place. Spending time at the busy courthouse made that easy to believe.

A few blocks away I found my car, then worked my way over to the Stevenson and took that to Lake Shore

Drive. I wasn't going directly home, though. Instead, I got off at the Belmont exit and kept going over to my office on Clark. It took about ten minutes to find a semi-legal parking place.

When I got to the second floor of my building, instead of turning toward my office I stopped in front of Madame Torneau's door. I knocked, hoping she wasn't with a patient or a client or whatever it is you call those who indulge in the power of suggestion. Not that I really cared, I was certainly willing to talk to her while someone lay there in a hypnotic state.

She opened the door and immediately smiled. "I've been expecting you," she said, as though I'd made an appointment. "Come in, please."

I stepped into her office just far enough to let her close the door. The room was homey, with an overstuffed sofa and easy chair, and an old roll-top desk. It always surprised me that her office didn't look more like a gypsy caravan. On that particular day, though, she herself looked quite like a gypsy. She wore a tiered peasant skirt with three different patterns and a solid red blouse that fell off her shoulder. I think the style was popular ten years before. She was probably a much younger woman when she bought it.

"Have a seat," she said.

"I won't be long. You sent Nello Mosby to me?"

"I did."

"So, why weren't you able to help him remember?"

"I'm not sure. If he was drunk or drugged at the time, then the events may not have imprinted, which would mean he couldn't access them. There may not be memories to remember. He said he hadn't much to drink, so he should have memories. Another possibility is that the memories are there, but they're too emotionally challenging to deal with so his subconscious mind is protecting him. And then, of course, he could be lying."

"Lying? He could be lying under hypnosis?"

"Yes. It's entirely possible."

"What would he get out of lying to you?"

"Well, he got a referral to you." She smiled—kind, friendly, annoying as shit. "He could be looking for attention. Someone to talk to when he's ready to tell the truth. I'm guessing, of course. I don't know why people do the things they do until they tell me."

"He broke up with a guy he's still in love with. Ty, I think. Did he talk to you about that?" I should have made Nello Mosby tell me exactly why he broke up with his boyfriend. I suppose it was the bereft look on his face that had stopped me. Unfortunately, I was going to need to know.

"He mentioned a breakup but he didn't really talk about it."

"Not even when he was under?"

"No. That wasn't what we were working on."

I'd had an uncomfortable experience with her a couple of years before. What I thought she was working on and what we worked on turned out to be different things. I wasn't sure whether to believe her.

"All right, that's all I needed to know."

Before I could walk out the door, she asked, "How are you?"

"What? I'm fine."

"The last time I saw you things weren't very good."

"Things are great."

"You're still smoking. I could help with that."

"How do you know I'm still smoking?"

"I walk by your office."

Great. I was stinking up the building. I'd have to remember to open a window every now and then.

When I got home, Joseph and Ross were both under blankets watching Peter Jennings on the ABC news. Ross was on the sofa and Joseph was on the floor surrounded by pillows. I didn't catch what Jennings was talking about because the show cut to a commercial for Empire Carpets. At the end of which, both Ross and Joseph sang the phone number with the commercial. "Five-eight-eight two-three-hundred. Empire." I got the impression they'd been doing it all afternoon.

"How's it going?" I asked, generally. Then more specifically, "Joseph, do you feel any better?"

"Kind of," he said.

"Not really," Ross corrected him.

"Do you have the flu?"

"Maybe. I'm not coughing. It's mostly in my gut."

"Did you take your temperature?"

"We don't have a thermometer."

How could I not have a thermometer? I wondered. But then I did a quick mental tour of the last few years. The police searching my apartment after Harker died, packing when I abandoned the apartment on Roscoe, paying one of the drunks from Irving's L Lounge to help me move what I could to my office, throwing away a lot of crap, then schlepping whatever I still had to this apartment. I guess it wasn't hard to see how a four-inch tube of glass might have gotten lost or broken or simply taken.

"Besides a thermometer, do you need anything?"

He shook his head. "I don't even need a thermometer. I'll be fine."

"Brian needs you to go over," Ross said.

"Why?"

"He said a social worker came by about Terry."

That didn't make sense. Terry was a teenager Brian and I kind of kept an eye on. He was also an emancipated minor so he didn't have a social worker. I asked the guys to order a pizza and said I'd be back in half an hour or so.

Brian's condo was on Aldine, just around the corner from my apartment. It was a courtyard building made of red brick the color of dried blood. He was on the third floor. It took approximately four minutes for me to get there and another four for me to climb the stairs and let myself in with the key I still had from the months I'd spent sleeping on his uncomfortable sofa.

"Brian? It's Nick," I called out as I walked in. I shouldn't have bothered; he and Terry sat at the dining room table. Brian had a glass of wine in front of him, while Terry slumped and sulked at the other end of the table. With his fluffy blond hair and peachy skin, Brian looked about five minutes older than Terry, who had already begun to count the days until he turned seventeen.

"There was a woman here," Brian said.

"I heard that."

"She said she was a social worker but she wasn't."

"I thought she was. She looked like one," inserted Terry.

"Go back and start at the beginning. Tell me what happened."

"I was just playing Pac-Man and the door buzzed. She said she was from social services, so I let her in."

"Okay. Why are you here and not at Mrs. Harker's?"

"She's sick."

"And he wanted to play Atari," added Brian. I suspected that was the more likely reason.

"What did she say her name was?"

"Rochelle LaRue." I didn't ask why he remembered her name. Rochelle LaRue sounded like a drag queen. I would have remembered it, too.

"What did she look like?"

"She had bushy red hair and big tits."

"Did she give you a business card or anything?"

"No. She had a clipboard."

"She looked the part."

"Yeah, that's what I mean."

"How old was she?"

"Old."

"Old like me or actually old?"

"Old like you."

"How long was she here?"

"Until Brian got back."

I glanced at Brian. "I started asking her questions and she said she had to leave. She said she was with Chicago Social Services, but there's no such place."

"No, there isn't. If she were legit she'd have said Cook County DCFS. Child and family services." I'd certainly had to call them enough back in the seventies when I was on the job. "And she would have shown an ID."

I looked at Terry and asked, "What did she talk to you about?"

The kid slumped a little more in his chair. He looked like he might burst into tears.

"Do you want a glass of wine, Nick?" Brian asked, probably to give Terry a moment as much to be polite.

"Sure, why not?"

He got up and went into the kitchen.

"It's okay, Terry. You didn't do anything wrong. This woman came to trick you. She's the one who did something wrong."

"She talked to me about Deacon DeCarlo. She said I didn't have to testify if I didn't want to."

"But you're not testifying."

"I told her that. She said I was wrong, she said that I do have to testify. And if I don't want to the best thing to do was to say I lied. That nothing happened with Deacon DeCarlo. That I made the whole thing up."

Brian was back with a glass of wine in time to hear the last. "Oh my God. You didn't say that before."

"Well, we know who she works for," I said. "She's working for DeCarlo's defense. She might be an investigator. Or she could just be some attorney's secretary. I'll have to find out."

"Am I going to have to testify?"

"You might have to. I'll try and find that out, too."

"I don't want to."

"I know. Go play your game, Brian and I are going to talk."

Terry jumped out of his chair and was in the living room in less than two seconds. It was the first normal thing he'd done since I walked in the door.

"Do you remember the name of the ASA who's handling this?" I asked Brian, as I sat down.

Brian opened a drawer in the built-in breakfront. He pulled out a manila file and set it in front of me. Inside was all the paperwork pertaining to Terry Winkler.

"Don't you want to keep this in a safe place?" I tipped my head toward the living room, indicating that I meant a place safe from Terry.

"He's an adult. Legally. He can look at any of this."

Of course, most of the things in the file were about a child who'd had shitty things happen to him. No one should have to look at that. Brian and I went through it together until we found a note he'd made that an ASA named Taylor Williams had called to say Terry would not have to testify.

"I'll try to find him tomorrow."

"Isn't this witness tampering?"

"If Terry's a witness. It might be."

"And if he's not?"

"They have a right to interview prospective witnesses."

"But she lied."

"We'll never be able to prove that. She'll say that she identified herself properly and that Terry agreed to talk to her."

"But that's not true."

I took out my pack of Marlboros and lit one up. Brian didn't really smoke, but he still had a nice crystal ashtray in the middle of the dining table. "It's not going to matter that it's not true." I lowered my voice, though I doubted it mattered, Terry was absorbed in his game. "He's not a very credible witness. It's easy to say he got scared and made up a story. That's what kids do."

I sipped my wine; it was very tart. "Don't worry, I'll take care of it."

"How's Joseph?"

"He's got a stomach thing." He'd asked about my boyfriend, now I had to ask about his. "And Franklin?"

"He's with his straight best friend. They're picking out a diamond ring for the guy's fiancée."

"That's romantic."

He shrugged, then asked, "How do you think Ross is doing?"

"Pretty good. He's eating more. Walking more. And he seems in good spirits."

"Do you think...? I mean, they're not sure everyone dies."

"I think he spent a year without much in the way of medical treatment. It's not a surprise that he's getting better with care." I didn't think it was a good idea to give Brian false hope. Yeah, I wasn't a doctor, and maybe he was right. Maybe not everyone died of AIDS. But if Ross were going to live, it wouldn't be because we hoped for it or believed in it enough. It would be because that's the way things worked out.

"Joseph told me about your Friday nights."

"Did he?"

"I hope it's okay he told me."

It wasn't really okay. I'd have preferred we keep that to ourselves. And whoever else happened along on Friday evenings. "Do you think Franklin would go for something like that?"

"No, he wouldn't. He'd never cheat on me. Even if I told him to."

I almost reminded him that Joseph and I weren't cheating on each other. But the wine was making me tired so I didn't bother.

"There may be a test next year. For the HTLV-III virus. They're going to be able to tell who's going to get AIDS and who's not."

"Do you want to know?" I asked.

"Everyone says it the responsible thing to do."

"But you're not sure?"

"No. I'm not."

We were quiet a moment, before I said, "It would feel like someone telling you the day you're going to die."

Chapter Four

I slept like crap. Joseph tossed and turned in his sleep, keeping up a dialogue with God knows who the entire night. Actually, it might have been God he was talking to. I couldn't be sure.

"Are you going to be all right?" I asked in the morning.

"It's just a flu. My temperature's only ninety-nine point nine. Not serious."

"Wait. I thought we didn't have a thermometer?"

"Ross found it while you were at Brian's. It was in a shoebox with a bunch of shaving stuff, cologne, a toothbrush. It was shoved in the back behind the towels." Harker's stuff. Things that were impossible to throw away and impossible to keep.

"Okay."

I felt weird. I should have been the one to do that. I should have found the thermometer. Or bought a new one. And at the same time, that shoebox, I should have thrown it all away long ago.

"Um, so that box—"

"Don't worry about it. I had Ross put it back where it was."

"Thanks."

I really couldn't think about that. I could barely think about Joseph being sick. After Harker, and Ross for that matter, it was hard to think about anyone being sick without it being serious. But he was right, healthy people got sick all the time and then got better. It wasn't serious. He'd be fine in a day or two.

I opened the front door and grabbed the paper out of the hallway. Below the fold was a pretty accurate drawing of ASA Sanchez giving her opening remarks. I turned on the burner underneath the teakettle and sat down at the little table with the paper in front of me. *This is what it's about*, I thought. The reason the trial had progressed despite the weakness of the State's case. Sanchez was turning herself into a courtroom star. There were few downsides for her. If she won she was a heroine and if she lost she could blame the CPD or the Feds or the unfairness of a system that allows the defense to outspend the prosecution—though it was the other way around 99% of the time. The thing she wouldn't have to do if she lost was blame herself.

The water began to boil and I made a really lousy cup of coffee in the two-cup metal sort of percolator. Ross was fast asleep. I think he'd stayed up late watching TV. I wished I could stay home and just keep an eye on both Ross and Joseph. I spread some peanut butter on a piece of bread, washed it down with thin coffee, scanned the rest of the front page and then went to shower.

Court was set to begin at ten, but I had something to do first. I got down to 26th and California around nine and spent ten minutes trying to find a legal parking spot. The parking lot at the courthouse was so small it was reserved for judges, prosecutors and their witnesses. There were a couple of pay lots, but they cost around eight bucks for the day and I was too cheap to pay it.

I found a space on a side street off 25th and walked back down to the courthouse. I didn't go in though. Instead I continued down to the concrete and copper-tinted glass mid-rise next door. The state's attorney had offices there.

After checking the directory in the lobby, I went up to the eighth floor and wandered around until I found Taylor Williams' office—well, desk is more accurate. The floor was divided into a maze of cubicles. I found a secretary sitting at a desk that seemed to service four or five of the cubicles. Her area was stacked with files and surrounded by boxes. Wedged in among the files was a computer that was probably only a few years old but already seemed outdated. The girl was in her mid-twenties, had too-pink skin and a bad case of acne. It was only around nine-thirty and she looked ready to burst into tears.

"I'm looking for Taylor Williams."

"She's going directly to court this morning."

She? Brian must have forgotten that. Or she had a very deep voice. I pulled a business card out of my wallet and handed it to the girl.

"My name's Nick Nowak…"

"Yeah, that's what it says here. We don't need private eyes. That's what the police do for us."

"This is actually more a personal thing."

"Oh." She brought her voice down low and said, "She doesn't date white guys. If you ask me that's racist, but don't try to tell her that. She'll go ballistic."

"It's about the DeCarlo case. I'm a friend of one of the victims."

That earned me a funny look. Not surprising. I was a little old to have friends in high school.

"That's not her case anymore."

"Oh, whose case is it?"

She frowned at me and moved a couple of files on her desk. She had a big piece of plexiglass as a blotter and had slipped pieces of paper with important information beneath it. One of the pieces looked to be a list of who had which case. She ran a finger down a column and then said, "Stork. Tony Stork."

"Really?" I could have wandered right off to find Tony, but it bothered me that it was now his case. "How long has it been Tony's case?"

"Couple months, I guess."

"Ms. Williams was too busy to handle it?"

"They're all too busy."

"So why'd she drop it?"

"It's a loser. She hates losers."

"How did it end up with Tony?"

"I don't know. I don't go to those meetings. Do you know Tony?"

"We've met. Can you tell me how to find him?"

"He's on the other side of the floor." She pointed behind me.

"Thanks."

It was one of those buildings with a central core that included the elevators, janitorial rooms, restrooms, heating and cooling ducts, wiring and just about anything else that was common to all fifteen floors. Around that core, the ASAs had put in bookcases filled with law books that they obviously shared. I was pretty sure it was close to ten, so I wasn't sure I'd have much luck finding Tony but when I got around the central core, I saw him coming toward the elevator.

He carried a briefcase in one hand and a stack of manila files in the other. He smiled when he saw me. "Look who's ventured into enemy territory."

"I need to talk to you."

"I hope it's personal."

"It's not."

"Bummer." I glanced at his left hand. It still had a wide gold band on his ring finger. I doubted he and his wife had the kind of arrangement Joseph and I had.

"I just found out you're on the DeCarlo case. How did that happen?"

"We need to walk and talk," he said. Stepping over to the bank of elevators, I hit the down button so he didn't have to. "We shift cases around all the time. Not a big deal."

An elevator popped open behind us. There were a couple men in it. Both in gray suits.

"I do remember seeing your name in the file," Tony said with remarkable blandness.

"One of the victims. He's an emancipated minor now. A friend and I keep an eye on him. Terry Winkler."

"Okay. I don't remember the name. But we're five or six months from trial on that one, aren't we?"

"I don't know. I haven't been keeping up. The last we heard Terry didn't have to testify."

"If he's a victim, why isn't he testifying?"

I didn't want to say that he was gay or that he enjoyed giving blow jobs in front of the gray suits, so I said, "He's precocious."

The elevator opened and we were on the ground floor. We walked through the lobby and out to the street. "When you say he's precocious, you mean he's a lousy witness."

"That too."

"All right. I'll try not to call him."

"Yeah, thing is, a woman came by yesterday claiming to be a social worker and spent some time talking to him about the case. We're pretty sure she was from DeCarlo's defense. She encouraged him to lie, to say that nothing had happened and that he'd made it all up."

"Okay, I need to get up to speed on this. I'll look at the file after court today."

"Do you remember who DeCarlo's attorney is?"

"Not off hand. And you really shouldn't be involved."

"Great. I don't want to be involved. The woman said her name was Rochelle LaRue. Which it's probably not."

We were walking through a glass tunnel that connected the administration building to the courthouse. Once in the lobby, we walked over to security checkpoint, Tony put his briefcase and files onto the X-ray machine. We waited in line to walk through the metal detector.

"If you're not busy at the lunch break, perhaps we could find an empty interview room."

He'd said it so matter-of-factly that it took me a moment to realize he didn't want to talk more about Terry. He was offering me a blow job.

"Sorry, wrong day of the week."

"That doesn't make any sense."

"I have a boyfriend. Fridays are our free day."

"Well, how about this week you be bad on Wednesday and good on Friday?"

"Doesn't work that way."

On the other side of the X-ray machine, he picked up his briefcase and his files. I offered to carry the files, but he declined. "It's not a good idea for you and I to walk into court together."

"That's probably true."

###

At about ten twenty, Jonathon Lidell took the stand. He was the scrawny bartender I'd talked to back in April, the bartender who'd told me he'd filed a complaint about Mickey Troccoli. He was also the owner of a bar called Dresden.

The day before, Owen had taken possession of the box I'd put together. It contained the interview Jonathon Lidell had done with the task force, the complaint he'd filed, as well as some basic background information, address—just a few doors down from where I'd lived on Roscoe—the fact that he was not married and probably gay, the fact that he owned his apartment and the building where the bar was located. Owen had reduced all of that to one typed sheet of paper. As ASA Sanchez began her questioning, Owen slipped the paper in front of Nathan Babcock.

"Tell us what your business is, Mr. Lidell," Sanchez asked.

"I own a nightclub called Dresden. It's on Belmont near the Jackson Howard El stop."

"Now, Mr. Lidell, you filed a complaint with the Cook County Liquor Commission in April of 1983. Is that correct?"

"Yes. It is."

"The complaint alleged that you were forced to buy substandard supplies at inflated prices from Agnotti Fixtures."

"Yes."

"Can you tell us about that?"

"A thug by the name of Mickey Troccoli came in shortly after we opened. He told me that I'd be buying supplies from Agnotti Fixtures. He showed me a list of things they sold. I asked to see samples and he got bent out of shape. A couple days later he came back with some cocktail napkins and some plastic skewers. They were pretty crappy and not cheap, so I said I didn't want to do business with Agnotti Fixtures. He said I would if I knew what was good for me."

"And then what happened?"

"A few days later there was a fire in the dumpster behind the club. That was followed by a note that said, 'Do what's good for you.' The note was on one of their crappy cocktail napkins. I did what was good for me."

"You started paying off Mickey Troccoli?"

"Yes. I mean, we opened an account with Agnotti Fixtures. Whatever they sent we threw away."

"How much did you pay them every month?"

"They sent an invoice. Usually for just over a hundred dollars. But then Mickey would come in and ask for two hundred in cash."

"And you paid him?"

"Yes."

"Every month."

"I tried to stop. But this Mickey guy just came in more often."

"Threatening you?"

"Yes. I tried to explain that I wasn't really making that much money; that I couldn't afford to pay them even if I wanted. And I certainly couldn't afford to buy supplies from two different places."

"Thank you, Mr. Lidell."

ASA Sanchez walked back to the defense table and sat down. Nathan Babcock took his time shuffling some papers around. I glanced at the spectators. Rose Hansen and Beverly Harlington were there again, dressed to the nines. The Outfit guys sat behind them, dressed as they had been the day before, except their rayon shirts were in different colors.

Babcock finally stood up and smiled at Lidell. "Good morning, Jonathon. How are you?"

"Fine."

"Fine? You're not nervous?"

"A bit I guess."

"Trials like this can be daunting."

"Yes."

"I'm sure you want to be careful to say the right thing."

"Your honor, could you instruct Mr. Babcock to ask questions rather than simply comment," Sanchez said, not bothering to stand.

"No need, your honor. I was just attempting to be cordial." Of course, he was doing no such thing. Suggesting that Lidell might want to 'say the right thing' rather than telling the truth was his actual point. And it seemed to have worked. The jury was looking closely at Lidell, asking themselves if he was telling the truth.

"Now, Jonathon, have you ever met Giovanni Agnotti?"

"No."

"Really? Why is that?"

"What?"

"Well, you just testified that a salesman who worked for Agnotti Fixtures was filling out order sheets for you, sending you whatever he felt like, and then demanding money from you on the side. It never occurred to you to go and talk to his boss about that?"

"But... he's Jimmy English."

"Yes, that's a nickname he's been given. And I'm sure we're all aware of the rumors and the gossip."

"Yeah," Lidell said. "Of course I am."

"So, you thought that if you didn't buy Mr. Agnotti's cocktail napkins he'd leave a severed horse head in your bed?" Babcock made sure to step to the side so that the jury had a clear view of Jimmy, who looked like a kind, gentle grandfather.

"I didn't think exactly that. I thought something *like* that might happen."

"You own the building you're in, yes?"

"Yes, I do."

"So you had to have a fire inspection before you opened the bar."

"Nightclub. Yes, I had a fire inspection."

"You paid a bribe, didn't you? How much was it?"

ASA Sanchez bolted out of her seat. "Objection! Mr. Babcock is assuming facts not in evidence."

"Oh really? I thought it was common knowledge that the fire department demands bribes."

It was. The likelihood that Lidell paid a bribe to pass his inspection was around a hundred percent. The defense was banking on the jury already being aware of that.

"Mr. Babcock also knows that the witness does not have to incriminate himself."

"The ASA is welcome to offer immunity. I have no objection."

"And he knows that he's libeling the Chicago Fire Department without evidence of fact."

"Actually, if we let Mr. Lidell answer we might have evidence of fact."

"Your honor!"

"The objection is sustained."

"I apologize your honor," Babcock said quickly. "I was just curious as to the going rate for a fire inspection." Everyone laughed at that. Except the judge.

"Your honor. The State requests that the jury be instructed to disregard this line of questioning. We also request that Mr. Babcock be sanctioned for his behavior." Neither actually sounded like a request.

Judge Corwin frowned deeply. It was as though he was a parent and ASA Sanchez had just told him how to discipline his child. If he'd been planning to do anything, he certainly wasn't going to after she demanded it.

"Could you just move on, Mr. Babcock? I think you've made the point you wanted to make."

"Of course, your honor. I only have one more question. Approximately two months after you filed a complaint with the Cook County Liquor Commission you were interviewed by someone from the CPD. Could you tell us the name of the officer who interviewed you?"

Sanchez practically elevated out of her chair. "OBJECTION!" She stopped. Now she was left with a dilemma. Talk of Devlin was excluded. But, if she made a point of that, the jury would begin to wonder why. Which was exactly why Babcock had asked. Sanchez rallied, "This entire line of questioning is nothing but fishing. Fire inspectors, interviewing officers? They have nothing to do with this case."

"Really?" Babcock jumped in immediately. "How can the name of the interviewing officer not be relevant to this case?"

"Your honor," Sanchez nearly whined.

"Just the name, Mr. Babcock, no more."

Babcock turned to Lidell and asked again, "What was the name of the officer who interviewed you?"

"Devlin. Captain Devlin."

Chapter Five

After another lunch of chili and oyster crackers, I made a beeline for my favorite bank of phones to make a few calls before it was time to go back into court. My first call was to check on Joseph.

"How are you feeling?" I asked, after we said hello.

"I'm doing better."

He didn't sound better.

"Don't lie to me."

"A little better."

"Okay."

"Brian's here. He brought cinnamon rolls from Ann Sather. Ten of them. Ross had a half a one and then Brian finished it. I might eat the other nine."

"Ah, then you *are* feeling better."

"I won't actually eat them, though. I don't want to get fat."

"You can get fat." I looked around to make sure no one was close when I said this, "I'll fuck you fat."

"Ah, Nick, always the romantic."

"I can't help it. It's my nature."

"How's the trial?"

"Nothing too exciting. We had three different bar owners this morning." And Babcock had asked them each who interviewed them at the end of their testimony. Devlin. Each of them was interviewed by Devlin.

"What's happening this afternoon?"

"You're entirely too interested in this." Mickey Troccoli was scheduled to be the next witness. It was stupid, but I felt weird talking about him with Joseph.

"Fine. Don't tell me. Brian brought movies. We're going to watch *Cujo* and then *Christine*. I have the feeling by six o'clock tonight I'll never want to own a car or a dog."

"You don't need a car, I have one. And with three of us in six hundred square feet a dog's probably not a good idea. I have a couple more calls to make before I go back upstairs. Tell Brian I talked to the ASA who's handling the DeCarlo case and told him about the fake social worker."

"The social worker was fake?"

"Yeah, Brian will tell you about it. I love you."

"I love you, too, you big secret keeper."

"You were asleep when I got back last night," I said, defending myself. Though, it was hardly Joseph's fault. I'd stayed drinking with Brian longer than I'd anticipated and had eaten cold pizza in front of the fridge while he and Ross slept.

"All right, go."

I said goodbye and hung up. I took out the remote to my answering machine and called my office. I couldn't quite get the hang of hitting the button on the remote at the exact right time, so I had to call back twice before I managed to retrieve my messages. There were two. The first was from Vincent Renaldi. He'd called on Monday. It was Wednesday and I hadn't gotten back to him. "Nick, can you call me back?" He sounded a little frantic. He'd fired me almost two years before. Yes, I hadn't been doing my job so I deserved to be fired. Which was the only reason I was planning to call him back. On the other hand, he'd fired me so I was in no rush.

The second call was Nello Mosby. "Mr. Nowak, um, my ex-boyfriend called me. I told him I hired you to find out what happened Friday night. He said he'd talk to you. You should call him. He said he could see you tonight."

I hung up the phone. There was something off about Nello's boyfriend wanting to talk to me. If he knew what happened Friday night, why not just tell Nello? And if he didn't know anything why make a point of talking to me? I mean, sure, I wanted to talk to him I just hadn't expected him to want to talk to me. That was the part that was weird.

I got out the piece of paper with Ty's name on it, tossed another quarter into the phone and dialed. When the phone was picked up, I said, "Hi. This is Nick Nowak. I'm looking for Tyrone Carter."

"Yeah. That's me."

"Nello Mosby left me a message saying you're willing to talk to me?"

"Yeah, sure, what do you want to know?"

"I want to know when I can come by and see you. I can't do this over the phone right now."

I didn't have a lot of time and I wanted to look him in the eye. He took a long time deciding to answer. "All right. I live at 1127 Keystone."

"Where is that?" I asked.

"It's near Division. West Humboldt."

I wasn't all that familiar with Humboldt Park. I was pretty sure I'd heard it had once been a Polish neighborhood, but then my family said that about almost every neighborhood in Chicago. Now I was pretty sure it was now Puerto Rican or Mexican and maybe a little bit black. I wrote down Tyrone's address on the same sheet with his phone number, told him I'd come by later in the afternoon, then I went back up to the sixth floor.

When I walked back into the courtroom, Owen hurried over to me. "Have you talked to Mickey Troccoli?"

"Not since summer. Was I supposed to?"

"No, no… it's just that I don't see him anywhere."

I looked around the courtroom and I didn't see him either. There was something wrong about this situation, but I wasn't sure what. "He's testifying next, right?"

"Yes, darling, he is."

"And Babcock is going to get him talking about Devlin?"

"That's the plan." I didn't know it for sure, but I had the feeling Mickey had taken a trip to Rawson Street Station and various unpleasant methods had been used to encourage his statement. I figured Owen's plan was to get Mickey to bring some of that up on his own.

"When did you talk to Mickey?" I asked.

"Ages ago."

That confused me. In August, I figured out that Mickey had talked to Operation Tea and Crumpets. I warned him that I'd have to tell Jimmy and shortly after he disappeared. When that went down, Owen hadn't seemed too sure who Mickey was.

"Ages ago last spring or ages ago last month?" I asked.

He gave me a curious look but didn't answer because the bailiff told us to rise as Judge Corwin re-entered the courtroom. The Judge sat down and so did we.

Everything got strangely quiet and then ASA Sanchez pushed her chair back and stood. "Your honor, our next witness is Michelangelo Troccoli. Unfortunately, we've been unable to locate him. We believe he's somewhere in

Las Vegas, but that's as much as we've been able to establish. At this time I'd like to call a witness who can testify to a statement Mr. Troccoli gave to the task force in the spring of 1983."

Owen poked Babcock and he, too, stood up. "Your honor, in the United States there's something called the Constitution which guarantees my client the right to face witnesses against him."

"The State would like to draw your honor's attention to rule 804(a)(5) and 804(b)(3), this is the hearsay exception we're relying on."

"And we rely on the Sixth Amendment."

ASA Sanchez picked up a sheaf of papers. "The State bases our position on Douglas v. Alabama and Bruton v United States."

"Your honor, there's no need to cite case law. We're happy to give the ASA time to find her witness. Perhaps a continuance is appropriate?"

The judge looked up, a bit confused. "Oh, you are, are you?"

Sanchez continued, "We've already been looking for Mr. Troccoli for a month."

"And yet he was on the witness list you gave us last week," Babcock pointed out. Apparently you were only supposed to list witnesses you could produce.

"We've been looking for him right up to the last minute."

"Ms. Sanchez," the judge said, drawing attention his way. "You can have a continuance if you'd like. Unless you've given up all hope of finding the witness."

"I'm afraid we're at the end of our rope. We're certain he's in Las Vegas. We're just not sure he's still above ground."

"YOUR HONOR!" Babcock yelled. "That is extremely prejudicial. This is a murder trial; to suggest that one of the State's witnesses has been murdered in front of the jury without even a shred of evidence is completely inappropriate."

"Jury will disregard," the judge said without enthusiasm.

Babcock sat down. It's hard to sit down with fury, but somehow he managed it.

"I think we can move on from the issue of a continuance. Who would you like to call next, Ms. Sanchez?"

"FBI agent Leonard Winstead."

"Sidebar, your honor," Babcock said, though he was ignored.

Sanchez rushed ahead, "Agent Winstead is part of the task force that investigated Jimmy—Mr. Agnotti. He's familiar with Mickey Troccoli's statement. He can testify—"

"You misunderstood, Ms. Sanchez. I'm not allowing hearsay in my courtroom on such flimsy grounds. You can have a continuance to find your witness or you can move on to other witnesses."

"Sidebar, your honor," Sanchez said.

This time the judge motioned them both forward. There was a small desk fan on the judge's bench. He flipped it on so that the rest of us couldn't hear the hushed conversation. I took that time to study the jury. They were certainly an unremarkable bunch. Six of them were white. Four black. Two Hispanic. The alternates were also mixed. There were eight women and the rest men. A half dozen were seniors, one nearly as old as Jimmy. I wondered what they were thinking of this mess.

Judge Corbin shooed the lawyers away and turned off his fan. "All right." He chewed his lip, thinking. "We will adjourn for the day. Honestly, listening to the two of you is giving me a headache. I would like written motions from both sides in my office by nine thirty tomorrow morning. We'll meet at ten thirty and I'll render my decision." He slammed his gavel and then hurried out of the courtroom like he hadn't wanted to be there in the first place.

Babcock leaned over to Jimmy and started talking quickly. That left Owen at loose ends, so I stepped over to him and said, "What do you need me to do?"

"We may need you to go to Las Vegas."

"Did you know Mickey was in Vegas?"

He glanced around and lowered his voice. "Of course I did. Sanchez is lying when she says they've been looking for him for a month."

"Do you know where he is now?"

"Alas, I don't. He was at Jimmy's hotel beginning at the end of August right up to last week. Then he disappeared."

"You don't think Sanchez found him and has lost him somewhere in the system?"

He glanced across the room and watched the ASA packing her suitcase. "It's possible," Owen whispered. "If we send you to Vegas you'll need to check the county jail."

"If he was at Jimmy's hotel she could have easily found him."

"Absolutely. That's how I know she hasn't been looking for a month. He's only been hard to find for a week."

"Did he check out of the hotel? What's it called? Lucky Days?" I'd come across the name of the hotel and casino in the files that had been my main employment for most of the year.

"Yes, that's it," Owen said. "Lucky Days. Did he check out? No. But then he might not have bothered. He wasn't paying for the room."

"Why haven't you been straight with me about this?"

"Oh, darling, I'm not straight with anyone," he said, making a joke out of it. "Sorry, I couldn't resist. I can't tell you everything because you're on a need-to-know basis. I'm sorry, but it has to be like that."

I gave him a mean, cold stare.

He leaned in close and said, "Stop being sexy. We're in public."

"I don't like not knowing things."

"Nick, it's my job to keep secrets. You know, maybe that's why you and I never worked out."

There were all sorts of things wrong with that and it was pissing me off. We'd fucked a few times and it had been fun. Neither one of us had ever hinted there might be more. He'd just tossed that out to distract me. We were on the same job. Legally, he could share with me. Whatever I did for Jimmy's case was privileged. On the other hand, if it didn't directly relate—shit, maybe he was right. I hated that. I hated that he might be right.

"If you don't need anything else, I'm going to take off."

"We're set, thank you. See you in the morning. Pack a bag, just in case."

Cars in Chicago generally don't hold up long. There were half a dozen dings in Harker's Versailles that had shown up after I started driving it around. I pretended not to see them. That was the reality of the city. Cars didn't stay new long. When I got out to Keystone, the auto landscape was decidedly worse. As I drove up and down Tyrone's block, I don't think I saw any cars made in the eighties. Most were early seventies, some were from the sixties and a couple dipped back to the fifties. None of them were what anyone would call cherry. A few were up on blocks.

Of course, the shabbiness of the neighborhood cars was far exceeded by the houses. It had once been an interesting block, clearly developed by a single builder. Each house was a story and a half, brick, and featured a funky roof that reminded me of barns I'd seen in Saturday morning cartoons. There's probably a word for that kind of roof, but since I'm not an architect I don't know it. Basically, the roofs had an extra angle in the middle of each side. With all the little houses in a row it looked like a toy town, and I half expected a giant toddler to show up and start squashing things.

Not that it would take much. After I managed to park the car, I walked by three houses that were boarded up before I found 1127. Those houses were covered with graffiti, as were many of the ones that were still occupied. When I got to Tyrone's house, it was like the others except someone had painted over the bricks in white. It had a cement stoop, two front windows, and a single window on the second floor. As I walked up to the front door, I realized the white paint was a strategy to combat the graffiti. I could see—just under the white paint—that someone had tagged the front of the house with a crowned king, kind of like from a playing card. There was an ornate L on one side of him and a K on the other. Whoever owned the place was trying to reclaim the house from the shit the neighborhood had fallen into.

I knocked on the door, waited, was almost ready to knock again when it opened. Tyrone Carter stood there. About five foot five, he was dark-skinned, with black hair in glossy curls that looked almost wet. He wore a baby blue tracksuit with floppy white socks.

"You that guy?" he asked, glaring at me through bloodshot eyes.

I offered him a business card and said, "Nick Nowak."

"I thought you were coming later." He ignored my card and walked back into the house.

Following after him, I said, "Sorry, things got shifted around."

He shrugged. "Better this way. My mom's at work. She don't like white guys much. No offense."

"I'm not offended." I figured it was fair. There were a lot of white guys in the world who wouldn't like his mom. Tit for tat.

We stood in the living room. It was neat and orderly, filled with cheap but well-cared-for furniture. There was a big console TV tuned to a soap opera. I think it was the one where the girl fell in love with her rapist and everyone thought that was romantic. Of course, that's probably not the weirdest thing that ever happened on a soap opera.

Tyrone got onto the sofa and curled up under a blanket. He didn't offer me a seat, so I didn't take one.

"Are you sick?"

"Stomach thing."

"Yeah, my boyfriend's got that, too."

He gave me a suspicious look. Either he didn't believe I had a boyfriend or he didn't think my boyfriend was sick. "Nello wants me to tell you what happened Friday night."

"Why not just tell him?"

"I did tell him. Now he wants me to tell you."

"Okay, go ahead, tell me."

"I was at Jay-Jay's around nine. Nello was there. We had a fight. I left and came home."

That didn't make much sense. Jay-Jay's was a dance club, so their being there at nine o'clock didn't make sense. And Ty's coming home after the fight didn't make sense either. An angry gay guy goes out on a Friday night.

"Why were you there at nine? That seems early for a place like Jay-Jays."

"There's no cover until ten. If you're inside already they don't charge. Me and my friends go at nine."

"When did you and Nello break up?"

"About a week ago."

"So a couple days before you saw him at Jay-Jay's?"

"Yeah."

"What did you fight about?"

"I was mad that he broke up with me."

"Are you still mad?"

"I suppose."

"Why did he break up with you?"

"Didn't he tell you?"

"Yeah, but it didn't make much sense to me." That was a better answer than no.

"It didn't make much sense to me either. Why are we talking about this? It doesn't make a difference about what happened to Nello on Friday night."

"What do you think happened to Nello on Friday?"

"He got drunk and can't remember. Big deal."

"Then why are his clothes covered in blood?"

"Oh, he told me that. I heard he had a nosebleed."

"Someone told you that?"

"Uh-huh."

"Nello said he's not prone to nosebleeds."

"So what? He can't remember, remember?"

I stared at him. He was lying and doing a shit job of it.

"Fine. Don't tell me the truth."

He looked shocked. Somewhere along the line, sweat had popped out on his forehead. He stared at the TV for a minute, watching a commercial for Riunite D'Oro, the wine that goes with everything.

"My friends don't like Nello. That's why he broke up with me. They pick on me for liking a guy who's high yellow."

"Isn't that a nasty thing to call someone?"

He shrugged.

"Maybe you need better friends."

"No shit."

Chapter Six

After I left Tyrone's house, I was happy to find that my car still had all four tires. West Humboldt Park was the kind of place that made me question my decision not to carry a gun. Yeah, having killed someone I didn't relish the idea of doing it again. Killing someone, even a bad someone, didn't feel good. It wasn't like in the movies where you kill someone and then in the next scene, you're back to looking for the nuclear codes or searching for the kidnappers or back undercover trying to take down the evil drug lord. No, in real life you feel shitty about it for a long time. Still, I was beginning to think that feeling shitty might be better than feeling dead.

When I got back to Boystown, I found a parking place two blocks from my apartment. I got out of the car, locked it, and then dug my Swatch out of my jacket pocket. It was nearly four-thirty. I put the watch back on my wrist so I could go into my building. It spent a lot of time in my pocket. It wasn't a bad watch. It was pretty simple, black and white. Joseph at least had enough sense to not get me a red or green one. Still, I didn't like the way it felt on my wrist. So far, I'd managed to be wearing it every time I came home to Joseph.

Brian was still there and the three of them were watching the end of *Cujo*. The drooling St. Bernard was attacking a Ford Pinto that held a little boy. Brian was in one of the director's chairs while Ross and Joseph were curled up at each end of the sofa. They looked a lot like Tyrone Carter. I worried for a moment that whatever stomach bug Joseph and Tyrone had was going to turn out to be something as bad as AIDS. Maybe there were so many people on the planet we were going to start spawning super bugs left and right. I pushed that thought aside. AIDS was making me paranoid.

"So what's the scariest thing in this movie?" I asked.

Joseph rolled his eyes at me. "The dog, silly."

"No, it's the bat that bit the dog," Ross guessed.

"You're both wrong. It's the freaking Pinto. If that dog hits it too hard it'll explode." Of course, I knew that wasn't where the dramatic tension was supposed to be coming from. But I did enjoy teasing them.

Brian tore his eyes from the screen and asked, "Did you find out anything more about that social worker?"

"No. If I do it's not going to be for a while. She's probably not coming back, though. How's Terry?"

"Glued to the Atari."

"Mrs. Harker is still sick?"

"Terry says she's got the stomach thing Joseph has."

I made myself a scotch on the rocks, found my beige princess phone and dragged it into the bathroom. I dialed and then lit a cigarette while it rang out in Edison Park. After three rings, Mrs. Harker answered the phone.

"Who is calling, please?" I don't think her phone rang very often. She seemed annoyed that it had.

"This is Nick. Are you okay?"

"Yes. I am very fine."

"So you don't have the stomach flu?"

"No. You have stomach flu."

"What?"

"Is what boy said. You have stomach flu, he need help out."

"Yeah. No, I'm fine."

"Silly boy. I send get well card. He get caught."

"Thanks for the card. I'll save it for some time when I'm really sick. Are you and Terry not getting along?" I used the sink for an ashtray, flicking my cigarette on the edge.

"We get along fine."

"Is he having trouble in school?"

"Boy is not good at school."

"No. He's not."

I was going to ask if she knew why he'd do something like this, but decided not to bother. So much had happened to the kid. It wasn't hard to imagine he'd need a break now and then. I had to figure that zoning out in front of a beeping TV screen was better than shooting up heroin.

"I'll make sure he's back with you tomorrow," I promised.

"Is good," she said and hung up on me. I sat in the bathroom for a while. Sipped my scotch, had another cigarette. Things were good but I still felt unsettled. My conversation with Owen hadn't made me happy. A professional lie was still a lie. Tyrone Carter was telling me lies. And now I find out that Terry has been lying. It felt like 'lie to Nick Nowak day.' That'd make a shitty national holiday, mainly because it happened a couple hundred days a year.

I dragged the phone back out to the living room. The movie had ended and the boys were talking about Chinese for dinner. I thought it was a great idea, but then I wasn't the one having stomach problems.

"Does Chinese work for you, Joseph?"

"Yeah, I think it might be okay. I'll stick to mainly rice. I am feeling better, Nick. I'm not even tempted to crawl back into the bathtub."

"Chinese it is then." I turned to Brian and said, "Mrs. Harker is fine. Make sure Terry goes back to her place after school tomorrow. Oh, and do you have a decent suitcase I can borrow? I might have to go to Vegas tomorrow."

After I told them as little as possible about my possible trip to Las Vegas, I lay down to take a disco nap. I'm not great at sleeping during the day, so it was mainly me lying there trying not to think. Trying not to think is not the kind of thing that works out. I was planning on a trip to Jay-Jay's, even though I had no idea how I was going to find out what I needed to know.

Around eight-thirty I got up and took a shower, made an attempt at shaving and splashed on some Polo. Joseph and Ross were watching *Dynasty*. I could hear them discussing the best way to adjust the rabbit ears to improve the picture, just the way an old married couple would. That made me hope Joseph would feel well enough to fuck soon. I'd like to remind him I was his boyfriend. Don't get me wrong, I liked that Joseph and Ross got along. But it had been almost a week since Joseph and I had done it. I was horny and grumpy.

After spending a couple years as the doorman at Paradise Isle, I had some idea how to dress to go to a dance club. Unfortunately, I didn't own any of the clothes I'd seen people wear. I threw on my jeans, my Nikes and an old blue and white striped rugby shirt. I pulled my corduroy jacket over the outfit. I wasn't going to dance, so it didn't matter much what I wore. It might be warm when I got inside the club, but I liked having pockets.

"Where are you going?" Joseph asked.

"I have a new client. Something happened to him last Friday at a club called Jay-Jay's. He doesn't really remember so I need to find out for him."

"Jay-Jay's? The black club on Halsted?"

"Why does everybody know about this place but me?"

"You're kind of set in your ways," Ross said.

"I wish that sounded more flattering."

He shrugged.

Joseph changed the subject. "Don't be out too late. If you're going to Vegas tomorrow, it would be nice to see you. I'll wait up."

"No, don't. You've been sick. You need your sleep."

"Well, then wake me up."

"Okay. I'll wake you up." I had no intention of doing that.

As I walked out of the apartment Ross and Joseph were trying to choose between *St. Elsewhere* and *Hotel*. It was a tough choice.

Twenty minutes later I was standing in front of Jay-Jay's, which was only seven or eight blocks away from my apartment. It still felt weird that I'd never heard of the place, but then it was pretty nondescript. At the point where Clark crosses Halsted diagonally, someone had built a pie-shaped building some sixty years ago. The storefront on the first floor had once been something like a five-and-dime. It had big glass windows divided by stone-faced columns. Except, some of the windows had been blacked out and some had been bricked in. The entrance was at the sharp end of the pie and had a small neon sign that said Jay-Jay's in pink. I could almost hear the music they were playing inside. It sounded like disco, but at the same time it didn't.

Sitting on a stool in front of the door was a very tall, very wide black guy. I glanced at my Swatch. It was still too early for a cover, if they even had one on Wednesday nights, so I figured he was just checking IDs. I took out my wallet, flipped it open and walked over to show him my driver's license. It was silly, of course; I looked well over twenty-one.

The big guy had a tiny flashlight and shined it at my license. Then he shined it in my face. I squinted at him and tried to look like myself. If the guy had been friendlier, I might have asked him a few questions about the previous Friday night. As it was, I figured if I said boo, he'd tell me I couldn't come into the club.

When he finally let me, I walked into the dark bar and it felt like I'd walked into a gigantic space, a world of its own. In the narrow part of the pie, there were a few café tables, then as the space widened, a dance floor, beyond that a long bar. On the east side, there was a staircase that went down to the basement. Hung on the ceiling were lights that flashed on and off and two mirror balls that threw colored specks of light everywhere. Even though it was still early, there were about fifty people. I wasn't the only white person; there were two of us. I might as well have had my own neon sign.

The music was loud and pulsing, with a beat that reminded me of a bratty six-year-old kicking a drum. I walked around the dance floor where ten or fifteen men were already dancing. When I got to the bar, I ordered a Johnnie Walker Red on the rocks and lit a Marlboro. As I paid the bartender, I realized Miss Minerva Jones was sitting at the far end of the bar with a short, round, little white man. The *other* white man.

Miss Minerva Jones had been the DJ at Paradise Isle. Given that she had a milk crate full of albums and two cassette-filled shoeboxes sitting next to her, my guess was she did the same thing here. She wore a platinum wig that made a big S across her forehead, pink lipstick, and a creamy sleeveless bodice dripping with glass beads. Since she was sitting at the bar, I couldn't see the rest of the outfit.

I took my drink and walked down to them. When she saw me, Miss Minerva tucked her chin and doing her best Scarlett O'Hara, said, "Well fiddle-de-dee, look who it is! Nick Nowak."

"Hello," I managed to say before she continued.

"Darling, it's been ages. I heard you became a Buddhist monk. Tell me that's not true." She turned on the barstool and I saw that she was also wearing a pair of lime green capris. Well, on her they were capris, on anyone who wasn't six foot five they'd be pants.

"That's not true. I did not become a Buddhist monk."

"Oh, thank heavens. It would be such a waste. Now let me look at you." She immediately frowned. "You're too thin. Eat more junk food. Little Debbies, Ho-Hos, Twinkies. Anything with artificial flavorings. And that shirt is so nineteen seventy-eight. Someone needs to take you shopping. Don't you have a queen in your life? A girl with some damn taste."

"I guess not."

"Well, call me. I'll take you shopping. By the way, this is Arthur Schmutz, the love of my life." It was a strangely perfunctory introduction. Arthur shook my hand. I said hey. "Arthur is a tax attorney. Give Nick your card, Sweetie."

Arthur and I traded cards, though I don't know why. I don't need a tax attorney and I can't image why a tax attorney would need a private investigator.

"I didn't know this place was here," I said, mostly to Miss Minerva.

"Why would you, honey? You're as white as Wonder Bread."

It didn't sound like a compliment so I skipped saying thank you. "Do you know a guy named Nello Mosby? Or any of these other people?" I slid the piece of paper Nello had written out in front of her.

"Oh honey, names are not my strong suit. Took me six months to remember your name. But then you white people all look alike." I think the last part was a joke. She couldn't possibly think Arthur and I looked alike.

"Nello is a kid around twenty-five. Black, but light-skinned. He was in here on Friday. Something bad happened. He doesn't remember what, but there's blood all over his clothes."

"I'm only here Wednesday nights and Sundays for the tea dance. However..." She hesitated dramatically. For a moment I wasn't sure she was going to continue. "There were a lot of rumors going around on Sunday. Something did happen Friday. A shooting, a stabbing, I heard both."

"And nobody called the police?"

"Oh, that is so adorable. Hope springs eternal. Honey, the police don't help black people; they arrest us. And if you're a black fag, well... calling 911 is suicidal."

"I wasn't like that when I on the job." Or, I tried not to be. I certainly knew officers who were. Shit, I was related to officers who were like that. "I get it, though."

"Have you been downstairs?" She tilted her head toward the stairs. "Shit go down. That's all I'm gonna say."

"Thanks." I almost walked away right then, but then I thought better of it. "What's down there?"

"It's a whole other bar. It's a whole other world."

I nodded, finished my drink and then walked across the bar to the stairs that led down to the basement. Of course, since the whole place was dark and windowless, you didn't have the feeling of going down into a basement. At first, it seemed just more of the same: more dark, more flashing lights, more thumping music.

There were almost as many people downstairs as there were up. The main reason the basement was smaller was that the point of the pie had been cut off and a banquette had been built across it like one giant sofa pushed up against the wall. The crowd was almost one hundred percent male, with the occasional over-dressed woman here or there. The look was showy. Silky polyester blend slacks and brightly colored shimmering shirts, fancy shoes, processed hair. Everyone was making an effort to get noticed. Except me. Which would have made me stand out if I hadn't been standing out already.

The bar itself was smaller and tucked under the staircase. Next to it was an opening to a hallway. I wandered over there, looking around, hoping anyone who cared would think I was looking for the men's room. The hallway was dark and longer than you'd expect. There were two restrooms on my left. On my right were three rooms marked private. I tried the first private room. It was locked. Then I tried the second door; it opened.

Inside, there was a built-in bench, similar to the banquet in the small bar. In front of that a low glass table. There were five guys sitting around. On the table, there was a small pile of cocaine and one of the guys was cutting lines with a credit card. I wasn't paying attention to the guys though, I was thinking about the room. Nello's clothes were covered in blood; that meant wherever that happened was also bloody. It might have happened in one of the private rooms. If so, who cleaned up the blood?

"Get the fuck outta here," one of the guys said.

"Yeah, sorry," I said and closed the door.

I went back out to the bar and pulled up a stool. The bartender was tall, thin and very dark. His hair was straightened and plastered down on his skull. There was a curl on his forehead that made him look very roaring twenties. Like I was in some speakeasy. And it wasn't too hard to imagine Jay-Jay's in the twenties: a five-and-dime upstairs and a speakeasy down. The bartender saw me and came over. He didn't look happy.

I laid two twenties on the bar and said, "I have a couple questions."

"Honey, I don't serve questions I serve drinks. You want a Crown and Coke? You want a Courvoisier and ginger? I'm your man."

"Did you work last Friday?"

"Awright, Courvoisier and ginger it is."

That sounded disgusting. I watched while he made the drink. He set it on a cocktail napkin in front of me. Then he picked up the forty dollars and put it into his shirt pocket. Great, forty bucks for a drink I didn't want.

"Somebody got hurt in one of those private rooms last Friday. Did you clean up the mess?"

"I don't do windows."

"You don't give straight answers, either."

"You don't wanna ask too many questions about what happens in those rooms. It just ain't a good idea."

"If someone was killed in here, you could get in a lot of trouble."

"You're crazy. No one died, awright? Just move on, there ain't nothing to see here."

"One more question. You know a guy named Evan Parker?"

"I know a lot of people."

"Is he here tonight?"

"Maybe he is, maybe he ain't."

There was a tap on my shoulder. I turned around and there was the doorman looking distinctly unhappy. It was time to leave. But before I did, I turned back to the bartender and said, "Thanks for the information. I have a much clearer idea of what happened now."

"I didn't tell you nothing!" he shouted.

"Totally worth the hundred bucks."

"I didn't tell you nothing and you didn't give me no hundred bucks!"

I turned back to the doorman and said, "Shall we go?"

When we got to the front door, the doorman gave me an unnecessary shove into the street. I crossed to the other side of Halsted and stood at the bus stop smoking a cigarette. Behind me was a very tiny Thai restaurant. They looked to be closing down for the night; it was maybe ten o'clock. I didn't feel like fishing the Swatch out of my pocket to be sure. I watched guys go in and out of the bar.

It would be nice to talk to Evan Parker. The bartender's "Maybe he is, maybe he ain't" made me think he was. I mean, why not just say no? Why play coy like that? Of course, there wasn't a way for me to get back into the bar and look around for him. And if he came out of the bar, I didn't know what he looked like. Still, I stood around waiting. I lit another cigarette. Then a third.

Waiting around paid off when a voice behind me said, "This may surprise you, but my favorite flavor is vanilla."

I turned around to find myself looking at J.J. from *Good Times*. Well, it wasn't J.J., but they did look a whole lot alike. He wore a pair of light blue slacks and a shimmering white shirt, both of which emphasized the deep, chestnut brown of his skin.

"Evan Parker?" I asked.

"Now how do you know my name?"

"Nello Mosby hired me to find out what happened last Friday. I'm a private investigator. Name's Nick Nowak."

"Well, Mr. Nowak, that makes you an asshole."

"Does it? Why?"

"Taking money from my friend Nello to find out what? That he drank too much and can't remember. He's not the first boy that happened to."

"He did wake up covered in blood."

"So somebody got scratched, big deal."

"Do you know who got scratched?"

He got a wary look in his eyes. "I don't actually know that. I was just guessing. I'm sure there are a hundred reasons Nello got a little blood on his clothes."

"It wasn't a little blood. It was a lot of blood."

"Is it human blood? Maybe it's not. Maybe someone was playing a practical joke like in that movie, *Carrie, Queen of the Prom*?"

He knew more than he was saying, but I figured I wouldn't be able to get it out of him. I switched tactics. "Nello said the two of you fought on Friday. What did you fight about?"

"He's not a drinker. I was trying to get him to slow down."

"What time was this?"

"Around nine I guess. I mean, if you're drunk at nine then what are you going to be like at midnight?"

There was something wrong about that. "So, Tyrone Carter says he was fighting with Nello around that same time. Did you fight with Nello before or after Tyrone did?"

"Tyrone wasn't there. He didn't get to the club until a lot later."

"How do you know that? You left after you fought with Nello?"

"I heard that Tyrone was there later on, that's all."

"What else did you hear?"

"Oh my lord, you can't be serious. The crowd in there, come Sunday afternoon they don't have anything to do but burn up the phone lines gossiping about Friday and Saturday nights."

"So what did you hear about Nello on Friday night?"

"That he was a drunk fool throwing himself at anything that walked. Gimme a cigarette, sweetheart. It's the least you can do."

I took my Marlboros out of my jacket and shook out a couple of cigarettes for us. I gave Evan one and lit us off the same match.

"Where did you go after you left Jay-Jay's? It was still early."

"I went to Big Nell's. I told you I like vanilla. You live around here, honey?"

"I do. Why do you think Tyrone lied to me about being in the club earlier?"

"Don't ask me, I can't read that boy's mind. Now, how about it? I live with my brother and he's got a girl coming over tonight. He don't want me to come home. What's your bed like? Is it wide?"

"It's occupied. My boyfriend's probably already asleep."

"You got a car we could fuck in? I mean, we can fuck in the alley but I like to explore other options first."

"Sorry. I have to take a pass."

He sighed dramatically. "Well, I need to wander off and find someplace to sleep tonight. Nothing terrible happened to Nello. You should give him his money back and tell him to forget it." With that, he turned around and walked away. I have to say his ass looked damn good in his tight pants as he went.

Sometimes I was sorry there weren't more Fridays during the week.

Chapter Seven

I was damp when I got to court. The closest parking space I could find was five blocks away. It was drizzling and barely fifty degrees outside. Not for the first time, I regretted that the case hadn't gone federal. The Federal Courthouse was downtown right near a stop on the Jackson Howard, not to mention right on three bus routes that went by my apartment. My life would have been a lot easier.

At ten twenty-five I took my seat. No one paid me much attention. Owen and Babcock huddled together, talking. They seemed confident in their motion, though. But then everyone at the ASA's table looked confident and serene. I figured confidence was a lawyer's trick. Though I wasn't sure why they bothered. The jury was noticeably absent. That led me to believe that whatever the judge was going to say he didn't want the jury to hear.

Mrs. Barnes sat next to me, as she had for three mornings. She hadn't said hello or spoken to me for any reason. She wore a sickly sweet perfume and I toyed with the idea that she might have died on the first morning. I mean, she was silent, motionless and gave off a gagging smell. It was a theory.

I looked over at the spectators, mainly so I could breathe in that direction. Jimmy's family was all in attendance. There was sketch artist in the front row. A couple of young guys who were probably reporters and my two friendly members of the Outfit.

Suddenly, the bailiff told us to rise and we all jumped up. Judge Corbin walked in and took his seat. We took ours. He cleared his throat and began. "This is a situation that makes me uncomfortable. The thing that became clear as I read your motions was that the state's attorney really does not want to call their own witness, eager to instead rely on his previous statements and putting forth dubious legal arguments to do so. On the other hand, the defense would like very much for this witness to be called or forgotten. While they stand on a firmer legal ground, I am deeply suspicious of their motives. In fact, I'm deeply suspicious of motives on both sides."

I thought for a moment that he might deny entry of Mickey's statement entirely, which would be a half win for Jimmy's team. There would be no connection, no bridge between Mickey and Jimmy, which would be good but not as good as telling the jury Mickey's words had been beaten out of him.

"For these reasons, I've decided to give whichever of you would like Mr. Troccoli to testify until Monday to find him. If he isn't in court on Monday morning I will read through Mr. Troccoli's original statement and decide if all or part of it can be read to the jury."

Immediately, ASA Sanchez was on her feet. "Thank you, your honor. I want to assure the court that we're committed to finding Mr. Troccoli. This is not the only prosecution of this nature he's—" She stopped as though she'd just made a mistake, then said, "He's a very important witness."

"Thank you, Ms. Sanchez. I've made my decision. Are there other witnesses you can put on the stand?"

"We feel it's important the jury hear from Mr. Troccoli or at very least hear his statements before we move on."

"Yes, I thought you'd say that. If there is no other business, court is adjourned until Monday morning at ten o'clock."

He pounded his gavel and court was over for the day.

Babcock gathered his things quickly. Jimmy's driver stepped forward and began to help the old man out of the courtroom. Owen said something to Babcock and then came over to me.

"Something big just happened, didn't it?" I asked, though it felt like a ridiculous thing to say since no one was acting like anything had happened. "When she said Mickey was a witness in another case. What did that mean?"

"I think she just put a price on his head."

"But I don't think Mickey knows anything about anyone but Jimmy," I kept my voice low so no one would hear me.

"That's probably true. But saying that in open court means Doves will hear about it. Doves can't always be sure what different people in his organization know and don't know. And it's a safe bet the State's Attorney, the Feds and just about everyone else are keeping tabs on Doves." I glanced over to see if the two Outfit guys were still there. They weren't. They were long gone. Probably already on a payphone calling Doves to tell him what was said. Owen continued, "We're definitely going to need you to go to Las Vegas, find Mickey and bring him back by Monday."

"That's a lot to do in one weekend."

"The only way he'll be safe is if we put him on the stand and he talks about taking a beating from Devlin. Once he does, nothing he's said anywhere will be believed. No one will be afraid of him. The price comes off his head."

"You lost track of him a week ago. Are you sure he didn't come back to Chicago?"

Owen chewed on that for a moment. "If he knew he wasn't going to show up for court, I don't think he'd come back to Chicago."

I didn't like the way he said that. "If he knew…" That meant Owen was thinking that something might have happened to Mickey. I sincerely hoped it hadn't.

"Give me a few hours and I'll check around."

"Why don't we give you the rest of the day? I'll have travel book you on a red-eye. If we messenger the tickets to your apartment is there someone there?"

"Yeah, there is."

"Perfect, darling. I think we're all set then."

I hurried out of the courtroom. In the hallway, Tony Stork stood chatting with ASA Sanchez. As I walked by he nodded cordially. It annoyed me, but I was in too big a hurry to think about it.

Minutes later I was rushing down California Avenue. Offhand, I only knew one place to check for Mickey. Drive-In Video. After that, I was going to have to figure out where he lived, though it was unlikely he'd go there. When I got to my car I was thoroughly damp again. I really need to throw an umbrella into my trunk.

Before I started the car, I decided to think this through. What are the reasons Mickey might not show up for court? That he was already dead. That he'd been arrested in Las Vegas and was being hidden. That he'd gone on the run and didn't want anyone to find him.

I guess it was possible that Mickey felt bad about ratting Jimmy out and couldn't face him in court. No, wait, that wasn't possible. He'd been staying in Jimmy's hotel for weeks. Mickey wasn't afraid of Jimmy. It was news to me, but they were now on the same side.

Shit, I really didn't know what was going on.

I drove out to Forest Park and found Drive-In Video. This was my third visit, and the third time I wouldn't be renting a video. I parked, hoping against hope that I'd be talking to Mickey's uncle rather than his cousin. His cousin was an annoying, useless little punk.

When I walked in, there were three or four renters browsing the shelves. Behind the counter was an older man with a comb-over that barely earned the name his hair was so thin. There was no line, so I walked right up to the counter.

"Help you?" the man asked.

"Are you Mickey Troccoli's uncle?"

"Yeah. You a cop?"

"I'm an investigator working for Jimmy English," I said to gain some respect. I handed him a card. "Do you know where Mickey is?"

"Jimmy wants him dead, doesn't he?"

"No, Jimmy wants him in court."

"Yeah. I'll bet. He broke the code. He talked."

"What if I told you he had to? What if I told you they were beating him to death?"

"If that's true, then he should have died."

"How long have you known that Mickey talked?"

"For sure? A week maybe. I had my suspicions." I doubted that. "I remember when he got beat up. It was more than a year ago. Said he got in a bar fight over some girl."

It took me a minute, but then I realized. A week. Owen lost track of Mickey about a week ago. Was there a connection? People find out Mickey snitched on Jimmy. Mickey disappears. Yeah, there was a connection.

"You haven't heard from him, then?"

"No. And he better not call me. I don't like what he done. It's starting to cause me a lot of trouble."

"Can you write down his address for me?"

Mickey Troccoli lived with his parents on a street called Nottingham. I wasn't sure what neighborhood I was in. I was directly north of Forest Park but back in Chicago. Mickey's block was just south of Roscoe. Which I guess was a funny coincidence since I used to live on Roscoe, only seventy some blocks east. The houses weren't all that different than the ones on Tyrone Carter's block; these had regular roofs but they were built by the same contractor. Brick and stone, one and a half stories, cement stoops, bay windows. Getting out of the Versailles, it occurred to me that the street looked like a row of half-pint milk cartons. The kind they give little kids at school to drink with their lunch.

Of course, the big difference between this street and the one in Humboldt Park was that none of the houses were boarded up, there was no gang graffiti, and there were no cars sitting around on blocks. The street had a lot of nice trees whose leaves had turned rusty and yellow. I didn't remember there being any trees in Humboldt Park.

Parking was plentiful since pretty much everyone in the neighborhood was at work. I found 3323 N. Nottingham about halfway down the block. The small brick house was faced in cream-colored stone, had a pert white-and-red awning over the front door and white wrought iron railings running up the cement stoop. I climbed the stoop and rang the bell. Nothing happened.

There were three Drive-In Videos. The first time I wanted to find Mickey I'd dug up the addresses for all three. The Forest Park store was the closest and I'd just got lucky finding Mickey there. If I remembered correctly, the other two were in Northlake and Franklin Park. My guess was that one or both of Mickey's parents managed one or both of those stores. At any rate, no one seemed to be home. Something his uncle probably knew when he gave me the address.

I looked up and down the quiet street. I would have been happy to talk to either of Mickey's parents, but since I couldn't I was going to have to be a bit more creative. There was a sidewalk on the side of the house that led to the backyard and the garage. I walked around to that side of the house. Fortunately, the house next door made it hard to see me. I checked all the windows on that side of the house. It was chilly so they were all closed. They were also locked.

There wasn't a lock on the gate to the backyard, though. I let myself in. Stuck on the back of the house was a wooden, glassed-in porch. There was a metal awning covering half the porch windows. It was red and white and matched the awnings in the front. I went ahead and tried the door. It was open. A wicker settee and a matching chair filled the porch. At the far end, the screens they used in the summer were stacked against the wall. I tried the back door but it was locked.

I had a decision to make, but it wasn't exactly a hard one. I was going to break into the Troccoli's house. I picked up the cushion off the wicker chair and held it up against the glass pane on the back door. Then I quickly elbowed it, breaking the large pane of glass behind it.

Given that Mickey's life was at stake, I didn't think his parents would mind so much about the breaking and entering.

Reaching through, I unlocked the door and went into the house. I had to move quickly, just in case any of the neighbors were home. I walked through the kitchen ignoring it, then I was in the dining room, which didn't interest me much either. In the living room, there was a large console TV with a VCR and a stack of brand new videos still in shrink-wrap. That also wasn't what I was looking for. Before VCRs, people used to decorate the tops of their TVs with family photos. I looked around the room. Early American living room set, maple coffee table, a set of bracket shelves on the wall. That's what they'd done with the pictures. I quickly figured out that Mickey was an only child. There were his grade school pictures, his high school graduation; those weren't much use to me. There was one photograph, though, that was what I was looking for. It was three by five; in it, Mickey—who was a good-looking guy with a clone mustache—was leaning up against his new Camaro, white with a T-bar roof and heavy red stripes on the hood. He was pretty proud of his car. It showed on his face. I took the picture out of the frame, folded it and put it into my jacket pocket.

The staircase was on the side of the house just as you came in. I hurried upstairs to find two small bedrooms with a bathroom between them. The first room I looked into had a neatly made double bed in the center of it. The parents' room. I hurried over to the other bedroom. There was a twin bed, a poster on the wall from *Saturday Night Fever*—Mickey must have been into disco or John Travolta or both—a four-drawer wooden dresser and not much else.

My first stop was the closet. Opening the door, I found that it was nearly empty. I flipped through the clothes in there and saw that most were from Mickey's disco past, as were the three pairs of platform shoes on the floor. There was nothing in the closet that he might actually wear anymore. I went to the dresser and began opening drawers. The top drawer was empty. Socks, probably. He'd taken all his socks. The next drawer was underwear. There were two pairs in there. Both were in the process of separating themselves from their waistbands. The remaining two drawers had been ransacked like the closet.

I stood up to think and noticed that there was dust on top of the dresser. Well, half the dresser. There was dust outlining a large rectangular spot. It was about the size of a VCR player. Next to the rectangle the dresser was covered in dust about halfway, then there was an irregular area where there was no dust. There'd been a VCR, probably with a small TV sitting on top of it. And next to that had been a row of Mickey's favorite VCR tapes. He'd taken it all with him.

What I was looking at raised a number of possibilities; actually more than possibilities, probabilities. Mickey had taken everything that mattered to him. When he left, he hadn't been intending to come back to Chicago. At least not in any permanent way.

The rest of the house was neat and well-tended. But Mickey's mother hadn't come into his room to dust even though it had been almost two months. Wait, was that true? What if he'd come back last week and taken his stuff.

I took a closer look at the dust and ran my finger along the spot where the TV had sat. It collected a new, less noticeable layer of dust. I was right the first time. Mickey had left two months before and his mom had been too upset to come into his room and clean. I didn't bother looking under the bed or flipping the mattress. I'd found out what I needed to know and it was time to get moving.

I was back in my car and driving away in less than three minutes. I was certain Mickey hadn't come back to Chicago, at least not intentionally.

Chapter Eight

It was after lunchtime so I grabbed a gyros, fries and an orange pop, then went to my office to eat at my desk. My mouth was crammed full of pita and spicy lamb when I pressed the button on my answering machine. There were two messages. The first was from Tony Stork.

"Nick, I took a look at the DeCarlo case. We've had a witness recant so we're probably going to use your guy. I'll need you to bring him in. Can you do it tomorrow? You know, since court's not in session? Give me a callback. I have a pretty open schedule." He left his number and hung up.

That was bullshit. Obviously, Tony knew I was the investigator for Jimmy English's case. He knew I'd be trying to find Mickey Troccoli. He was using Terry to throw up a roadblock. It wasn't going to work.

The second message was from Vincent Renaldi, which was annoying since he'd called the day before. He was desperate, but there wasn't much I could do for him since I was about to leave town. I looked at my Swatch; it was one thirty-five. There was a good chance Renaldi would be at lunch so I gave him a call.

"Peterson-Palmer," a receptionist said.

"Yeah, Vincent Renaldi."

"He's at lunch right now."

Good, I thought. "Could you let him know that Nick Nowak called?"

"N-O-W-A-C-K."

"No C."

"Oh. Okay. N-O-W-A-C."

Didn't I just say no C? I almost gave it another try but decided not to. "Yeah, that's right. Can you also tell him that I'm going out of town and won't be back until next week?"

"…won't be back until next week…"

"Okay, thanks."

I hung up and dialed Tony Stork. I hoped that he, too, would be at lunch and I could just leave your basic no-fucking-way message. Unfortunately, when I asked for him I was put through.

"Oh, Nick, thanks for getting back to me. What time can you bring the boy in tomorrow?"

"That's not going to happen, Tony. That's not enough notice. Next week sometime."

"Now you've got me raring to go on this one. And besides, tomorrow is Friday. I seem to remember that being an important day for you."

There was a leering "if you know what I mean?" hanging in the air. But I didn't have time for that and I really didn't want to tell him I was going to Las Vegas. He probably assumed it, but there was no reason to confirm it. "Which of the other boys dropped out?"

"I don't have the file in front of me. But I can tell you tomorrow."

"Look, why don't you worry about who's tampering with your witness? Once you get that straightened out I'll bring Terry in."

"You do realize I'm an ASA. I don't negotiate when and if I'm going to talk to witnesses."

"He's a witness in a case that isn't coming to trial for six months, about crimes that happened more than a year ago. If you try to pull anything, we'll sue your ass."

"I have other ideas about what I'd like you to do to my ass."

"Charming. I'll talk to you about Terry next week."

And then I hung up. That was a very short conversation in which Tony had managed to lie to me, threaten me, and flirt with me. That took a lot of skill. My guess was they'd be promoting him soon.

Joseph and I had fallen into the habit of checking in with each other at least once during the day. If he was out on a temp job he'd call me at the office or beep me. If I knew he was at home, I'd call him. He was my next call.

"What are you eating?" he asked after I said, hello.

"French fries. How do you feel?"

"Well enough to drive you to the airport later. A messenger brought a package from Cooke, Babcock and Lackerby."

"Did you open it?" I'd said I might be going to Vegas. I hadn't said it was definite.

"No. But it says Travel Department on the envelope."

"Go ahead and open it. Tell me what time I'm leaving."

I heard paper ripping in the background and then, Joseph said, "Uh, let's see. Yikes. You're leaving at one fourteen. A.M." Then he said, "Oh wow."

"What?"

"There's five hundred dollars cash in here."

"Good. Spending money." You could say a lot of shitty things about Jimmy English but he wasn't cheap.

"I'll say. Buy me a souvenir."

I didn't reply to that. It was a business trip. Maybe I'd have time to buy souvenirs, maybe I wouldn't. "When do we have to leave to make sure I get my flight?"

"At that time of night, it should be a quick thirty minutes to the airport. A few minutes to park, and then fifteen, twenty minutes to find your gate. We should leave around midnight so you've got a cushion. Have you never flown before?"

"No. I've been to the airport, though." Once, a very long time ago, I chased someone through the international terminal.

"But you've never been on a plane?"

"No. I'm a third generation Chicago Polack. All my relatives live within an hour's drive."

"What about vacations? Your family never went anywhere?"

"We went to the Dunes every year."

"Oh my God, you're a virgin."

"Don't sound so excited."

"Of course I'm excited. I didn't think I'd ever get to say that. You're a virgin."

"All right, enough. You know you don't have to take me. I could take a cab."

"No, I think I'll be up to it. And I want to."

"You just want to get your hands on Harker's Lincoln."

"You see right through me. Is the reason you're going to Vegas going to be in the newspaper?"

"It might be. I'm looking for a missing witness."

"But, didn't the trial just start? The prosecution goes first, right? Or was Perry Mason lying to us all those years?"

"It's complicated. Sometimes I'm not sure I get it. I think the simple answer is that the ASA wants half of this guy's testimony and the defense wants the other half. If I can't find him, then the ASA may get to read some of his statement into the record, which is the half they want."

"Okay, I kind of get that."

"So, I interviewed this guy yesterday who had the same stomach flu you have. I guess it's a twenty-four-hour thing."

"I don't know. I've been feeling off for about a week. The last few days have been the worst."

I guess that meant Tyrone would be feeling bad for a few more days.

"Okay, so I'm going to try and get a few more things done and then I'll be home. I love you."

"I love you, too."

A big part of me was nervous about the trip and all I really wanted to do was go home, pack and get to the airport. But I had almost twelve hours before my flight and there were still people I could talk to about Nello Mosby. I figured I could get to at least one or two of them that afternoon. Before I did that though I decided to take another look at his clothes. Nello had left the bag containing his bloodstained clothes from the previous Friday.

I laid the shirt and pants out on the floor in front of my desk. Maybe I should have been more careful. On the floor, they'd likely pick up fibers from my carpet and, though I couldn't leave fingerprints on cloth, grease from my lunch might be spreading itself all over. On the other hand, the chain of evidence on the clothes was already pretty messed up. Presumably, Nello had worn the clothes into one of the VIP rooms at Jay-Jay's, though I couldn't prove that and didn't know which one. I also had no idea where the clothes had been between the time they'd left Jay-Jay's and eventually ended up in my office. In a trial, they'd prove useless. Too many opportunities to be tainted.

I picked up each piece and looked at it. There was almost no blood on the back of the pants or the back of the shirt. It was all on the front. I looked closely attempting to decide whether there was any kind of pattern. Mainly the blood was on the lap area of the pants and the lower portion of the shirt. It was one big, irregular blob with a few spatters around its edges. It almost looked as though the blood was rubbed into the clothes.

And it smelled terrible. It smelled metallic, and spoiled, like the meat department at a grocery store you promised yourself you'd never go back to. But there was also another smell that was familiar enough, but it took me a moment to place it. I picked up the shirt and sniffed it. Bleach. From the last washing? Except, not bleach. I looked closely and saw that it wasn't only blood that was stiffening the shirt. There were stiff circular stains that, as a thirty-six-year-old gay man, I was all too familiar with.

The shirt didn't smell like bleach, it smelled like a cum-rag. When I looked closely I saw that there were stiff blobs of cum all over the shirt. They appeared to be beneath the blood. Was that right? There were places where blood split a dab of cum in half and other places in the blood that seemed to also have a cum blob. But which had gone down first? Both the blood and cum were a bit crusty. I could flake some off if I wanted. Not that I wanted.

I lay the shirt back down, sat back down at my desk and lit a cigarette. Someone hadn't just bled on Nello, they'd ejaculated on him. And given the amount of cum I saw on his shirt, and without even looking closely at his pants, I'd say more than one person had cum on him. How did that change things?

Something happened to Nello in one of the VIP rooms at Jay-Jay's. That something included at least a couple of someones coming on him and then one someone bleeding on him. This was the thing, though. Whenever I'd had sex with more than one guy, and there certainly had been those times, when that happened I always took my clothes off. All my clothes. Sex was just more fun that way.

I had a disturbing thought, set my cigarette in the glass ashtray I kept on my desk, and went back to Nello's pants. I didn't bother checking them on the outside, instead I turned them inside out and looked for cum. I didn't find any. Did that mean something? It could mean that Nello didn't have as much fun as the guys he was with. But then again, it might not. He could have opened his pants and taken his cock out. He could have even pulled his pants down around his knees. The slacks were a rayon and polyester blend; a herd of elephants could have stampeded across them and they wouldn't have shown a wrinkle.

I didn't like what I was thinking. I wanted to think that Nello had gotten very drunk and had some kind of sex with a couple of different guys and maybe a nosebleed. It didn't seem likely, though. It seemed a lot more likely that Nello had too much to drink—except he claimed he hadn't so maybe he'd been given something, a Quaalude? Two Quaaludes? And then a couple of guys, or a few guys, had taken advantage of him.

I wasn't sure if I was right but it was possible enough to make me pick up the phone.

"Nello? I wonder if we could get together. There's something I'd like to talk about."

"I'm getting ready for work. I'm on at three."

"Where do you work?"

"Melville's on Rush." I didn't know it.

"If I come down would have you a few minutes to talk to me?"

"You found something out? Um... you don't want to just tell me now?"

"I haven't found anything out for certain. I'd just like to ask you a few questions. In person."

"Okay. Can you pretend to be a customer?"

"Sure, I can do that."

"All right. Come around three fifteen."

###

Melville's was on State Street just before it joined up with Rush. I took the El down to the Chicago stop overshooting my destination by about six blocks. It might have been shorter to get off at Clark and Division but there was an errand I wanted to run before I saw Nello Mosby. Coming up out of the subway, I took a look at my Swatch. It was two-fifteen. I had plenty of time.

The 18th district station was about three blocks west of the El. I think I heard it once called the East Chicago Station, which was stupid because the address was *West* Chicago. I mean, the station was about eight blocks from the lake so it was east of most of the city, but still. The building the station was in was three stories of dirty granite. I had no idea how old it was, but I'd guess that if they tried to sandblast the granite back to its original white there'd be nothing left to hold it together.

Frank Connors, Harker's old partner, worked on the third floor. Even though I was getting a pretty good idea what happened to Nello Mosby the Friday before, I needed to be completely sure. I knew the where, I'd guessed the what, but the who was eluding me. I didn't know whose blood Nello had been covered in. Connors might be able to tell me if any random person had been picked up bleeding in the neighborhood.

When I got to Connors' desk at the back of the third floor I found a lanky black guy in his late twenties. "Is Connors around?" I asked, wondering who the hell this guy was.

"Out."

"When's he gonna be back?"

That earned me a shrug.

"Is he at a crime scene?"

I heard a throat clearing behind me and turned to find Detective Monroe White standing there. He was in his forties and had a tendency to gain and lose a lot of weight. I knew that, not because I knew him well, but because I recognized his suit. It was cheap and tan and he'd been wearing it when we met. It had been loose just two months before. Now it was tight. The stereotype about cops and doughnuts must be colorblind.

"I'm looking for Connors."

"He's not here."

"I've picked up that much. Where is he?"

"He's on leave."

"Oh. What's the matter with him?"

"Stress."

"Stress?" I asked. It was a stressful job but that was part of the deal.

"Yeah, black people stress him out."

Now it made sense. Connors had been partnered with White and it hadn't worked out. They must have tried sticking him with the young guy sitting at his desk. Apparently, that didn't go well.

"All right, maybe you can help me. I'm trying to find out if anything violent happened near where Clark and Halsted come together last Friday night."

"Read your newspaper. That'll tell you."

"You know a lot of crimes don't get reported."

"What kind of crime are you interested in?"

It was White's job to get more information than he gave. It was my job to protect my client. That meant we could go on all day trying not to tell each other anything. I decided to play my only card and see how things went down.

"I can't say much but whatever happened was bloody."

"I'd know if there was a murder. And there wasn't. Not there. Not on Friday. There's a fag bar right there, isn't there?"

"It's a black dance club."

"There you go. Someone got bashed. People don't always report that, you know." That made me uncomfortable. I'd been bashed a long time ago and hadn't wanted to report it. Not for the first time, I wondered how much White knew about me.

"You might be right. I just needed to be sure."

"Let's back up. You know something bloody happened and you have a vague idea where it happened. So, tell me why it is you don't know what happened?"

"I've gotta run. I've got an appointment I don't want to be late for."

"No, no, no...you're talking about a crime. If you don't tell me everything you know it's obstruction of justice."

"Listen, White, it's a fag thing. You want another fag thing cluttering up your desk?" The last one hadn't gone well for him. Nothing official happened to him but my guess was he'd gotten a stern talking to about the things that went down.

He gave me a cold stare for a few seconds then said, "Get the fuck out of here."

###

I was at Melville's in exactly the time it takes to smoke a cigarette. The place was on the first floor of an old residential hotel called The Chestnut. The building was set back from the street, which gave it about three times the normal amount of sidewalk. That space was filled up with café tables and chairs. The tables were covered with red-and-white check tablecloths. There were three wood and glass double doors that led into the restaurant proper. I imagine that in the summertime they were all flung open to catch any stray breezes.

The morning's drizzle had stopped, but the clouds were still thick overhead, and the air was cold and unsettled. I didn't think anyone would be sitting outside and couldn't image why they kept putting the tables out in late October. I went through the center double doors and found myself facing a hostess. She was in her late teens and had a baby face that made her look even younger. Her hair was long, blonde and ended with loose ringlets halfway down her back. She was busy organizing the long strands behind her shoulders when I got to her. She stared at me so I said, "Could I get a table?"

"For how many?"

"Just one."

She got a quizzical look on her face, like she wasn't sure whether to tell me no or not. I didn't see why it should be a problem though. The place was completely empty. Boz Scaggs was playing on a stereo somewhere, "Harbor Lights." It was from the seventies, I remembered it well.

"Smoking or nonsmoking?" the hostess asked.

"Smoking. And could Nello wait on me?"

She looked me up and down, thought about it, then

shrugged. "I guess. Follow me."

After leading me across the restaurant, she deposited me at a tiny table shoved up against the back wall. She dropped a menu on the table, rearranged her hair and said, "I'll tell Nello he has a table." I watched her wander across the restaurant to a swinging door upholstered in fake leather. She pushed the door open and yelled, "NELLO!" Then she let the door flop closed and went back to her station near the front.

Pretty quickly, Nello was standing there in a pair of black slacks, a white shirt, bow tie and a big white butcher's apron. He smiled at me in a friendly way and said, "Can I get you something from the bar?"

"Sure. I'll have a Johnnie Walker Red on the rocks. And you'll be able to talk for a minute when you get back?"

"Yeah. We need to pretend to talk about the specials. The girl who sat you, she's the owner's daughter."

"Okay. We can do that. I wouldn't want you to get in trouble for ignoring your other tables." I glanced around the empty restaurant.

He sighed and said, "I didn't say it made sense. I'll get your drink."

Then he walked over to the bar. It was a pretty nice bar, taking up one whole wall of the restaurant. A few minutes later, Nello was back with my drink. Setting it down, he said, "So, I guess you found out what happened last Friday? That's what you didn't want to say anything on the phone?"

"Not exactly, no."

"Then why are you here?"

"I have a couple of questions. First, when you woke up on Saturday morning what was your hangover like?"

"I'm not sure I even had a hangover. I mean, I was a

little sleepy." He drank enough to have a blackout but he didn't have a hangover. That was a problem.

"Did you pay much attention to your drinks?"

"I drank them. Isn't that paying attention?"

"Did you dance?"

"Yeah, it's a dance club. Why? Why are you asking about my drinks?"

"Look, there's something... I'm ninety percent sure no one was murdered. I don't even think anyone was seriously hurt. If something bad happened, I think you may have been the victim."

He looked confused. "That's not possible. I mean, I wasn't hurt. I looked, believe me."

I wasn't sure how to ask what I needed to ask. "Hypothetically, if you *were* the victim, would you want to know?"

"But I wasn't."

"It would help me if you answer, that's all. So, hypothetically…"

He didn't bother to think too much about it. "Yeah, of course I'd want to know. I don't understand why you're asking me this."

I didn't want to explain so I moved on. "I'm going out of town tonight and I won't be back until Monday."

"So you won't be working on my case."

"Not for a few days. If you change your mind and you decide you don't want to know just call my office and leave a message."

"You're making me uncomfortable."

Great. That's what I was trying to avoid.

"Forget about it then."

"I'm not sure I'll be able to," he said, morosely.

"Yeah."

Chapter Nine

I got home a bit before five. Part of me was counting down the hours until I got onto the airplane. Eight. And until I had to leave for the airport. Seven. Or maybe only six and a half. I was developing two fears at once. One was that the plane would fall out of the sky. Another was that I wouldn't make it to the airport in time to catch the plane that was going to fall out of the sky. I fervently wished that Las Vegas was within driving distance. I'd have left hours ago.

When I walked into the apartment, it smelled delicious. Ross was somehow managing to fry chicken in my Pullman kitchen, while biscuits baked in the narrow oven.

"We're having a going away dinner for you. Brian and Franklin are coming over," Ross said.

I glanced over at Joseph who was sitting in one of the director's chairs. He looked a bit healthier. Still, I walked over and checked his forehead. It felt normal.

"Will I live?" he asked.

"I think so."

"I'm surprised Brian isn't here," I said, to Ross.

"He was here. He left you a suitcase on the bed."

"I started packing for you," Joseph added.

"Oh. Thanks." I wasn't exactly sure I liked that. But, I was too glad he was feeling better to complain. I went into the bedroom and took off my jacket, laying it on the bed next to the suitcase. It would be going with me, of course, but I'd probably wear it on the plane.

Brian's suitcase lay open on the bed. It was hard plastic and baby blue. Samsonite. I was going to look lovely walking around with that. Joseph had packed four pairs of boxers, three pairs of tube socks, two pairs of black stretch socks, a tube of KY jelly and six condoms. Obviously, he was trying to tell me something. I was going to be in Vegas all of Friday. It was conceivable that I might need one or two condoms, but not six. I might need six, though, if we were going to count the entire trip as a Friday. And I got really lucky.

I threw a couple of T-shirts and a dress shirt into the suitcase. I'd think about the condoms later. Of course, I could ask Joseph what they meant, but then I'd know for sure he wanted the entire weekend free himself; I didn't feel like knowing that. Not for sure.

I tried focusing on what I'd need while I was in Las Vegas. Except I had no idea what I'd need. Was it hot there in October? I had no idea. Joseph came into the bedroom. He looked cute in his flannel pajamas. They were dark blue plaid and too short for him, letting his naked ankles show. The deep blue made the skin that peeked through even whiter. I wanted to peel the pajamas off him like a banana skin.

"Close the door," I said, moving the suitcase onto the floor.

"I don't know that I'm up for much. I'm better but not perfect."

I got onto the bed, saying, "Then just come over and cuddle for a while." I wanted to fuck him, but I'd settle for just touching him.

Joseph climbed onto the bed and slipped into my arms. I kissed him on the forehead and tucked his head under my chin. Of course, my cock began to stir almost immediately, but I just lay there, holding him.

"I thought you might be trying to seduce me," he said.

"I am. I'm just more patient than you think."

He chuckled. Neither of us moved. To take my mind off my stiffening dick, I said, "So, I told you about my client who can't remember."

"You said a couple of vague things. You don't like to talk to me about your work, remember?"

"Yeah, but I need help with this one."

"Okay."

"Pretend you're still a priest."

"I do every Sunday when I call my parents."

Joseph hadn't told his parents that he'd left the priesthood. They thought he was on an educational sabbatical studying Catholic refugees from Henry VIII in the archives of the Newberry Library. I'm not sure how possible that was but, the idea obviously appealed to his parents.

"Something happened to this guy last Friday. He doesn't remember because he blacked out. When he woke up his clothes were covered in blood."

"Okay, that would be scary."

"What he doesn't realize is that his clothes were also covered in semen."

"Oh. I see."

"I think he might have been drugged. And then some guys took advantage of him."

"Advantage? If the cum is on his clothes what are you thinking? Some kind of circle jerk."

"Or a round robin blow job. The fact that he was dressed makes me wonder if it was entirely voluntary."

"Because if he's into guys coming on him he'd want it on his skin."

"And if he's not into that, then why be the center of attention?"

"You're not sure if you should tell him. That's why you're talking to me about this, isn't it?"

"He doesn't remember. I feel like telling him might make the whole thing worse."

"He's better off not knowing, that's what you think?"

"Yeah. That's what I think."

"You might be right."

"So I shouldn't tell him?"

"No, you should tell him."

"Why?"

"Because it's the truth. And I don't know if it's your place to decide."

"Is that what you'd do if you were a therapist?"

"If I was a therapist, if I was still a priest, I think I'd try to guide him to understanding what happened on his own."

"That sounds like telling but not telling."

"Maybe. I'm just thinking he hired you to find out what happened to him, so he needs to find out. If you can think of a way for him to find out without your telling him, then you've done your job."

I hugged him closer. It was a nice idea but very unlikely. I mean, I wasn't going to send him an anonymous letter or tell Madame Torneau what happened and ask her to replant the memories. Eventually, I was going to have to tell Nello Mosby what happened. But not until I was sure. And I wouldn't be sure until after I got back from Las Vegas.

Despite the distraction, my dick was still hard. I rubbed it up against Joseph's belly.

"What are you doing?"

"Making sure you miss me."

Then I kissed him like there was no tomorrow.

In the end, I took a cab to the airport. Joseph still wanted to drive me and wait with me until my plane took off, but I pointed out that he'd be getting home around two in the morning. Parking in my neighborhood was a challenge in the bright light of day. At 2 a.m. it was nearly impossible. He'd be driving around for forty-five minutes at least, and he'd end up blocks and blocks away. I didn't like the idea of him walking around alone in the middle of the night.

I was happy I'd put my foot down, because when I called a cab at eleven-thirty Joseph could barely get out of the chair to kiss me goodbye. Ross was already asleep on the couch. Dinner had been pleasant. Franklin was making an effort to get to know Ross, which was amusing and annoying at the same time.

After he asked three leading questions about Ross' dreadful family in Normal, I couldn't resist. "So, who are you voting for Franklin?"

"I haven't decided yet."

Brian nearly spit out his drink. "You said you were voting for Mondale."

"I know, but I talked to some of my friends and they made very good points about Reagan."

"Your straight friends," I said.

"Yes, my friends are straight. Big deal. You can't deny that Reagan has done wonders for the economy."

"Not my economy," Brian said. "Now I have to pay taxes on my tips."

"But you should pay taxes on all the money you earn."

"And so should rich people, but he's giving them a huge tax break." Brian was in the unique position of being poor and rich at the same time.

"It's just good sense to do that. Rich people spend more money."

"That's not really true, Franklin. My grandfather was wealthy. He left the money to my father who left the money to my mother who left it to me. There's more money now than when my grandfather died. We've never touched the principal. We don't even spend all the interest."

I'd never really known how much money Brian had. I now had a better idea. Quickly I did some math in my head; a simple savings account paid seven percent, a CD eleven or twelve, and bonds were probably more. It didn't take too many millions before Brian was raking in money hand over fist. Franklin was a bit flummoxed by the response or he was trying harder than I was to figure exactly how much money Brian really had. Either way, he went silent.

I decided to turn the conversation a bit. "And, of course, you agree with Reagan on traditional values?"

Franklin looked at me uncomfortably. "I believe in having morals."

"But the man you want to vote for doesn't think it's possible for you to have morals."

"I didn't say I *was* voting for Reagan. I said I was *thinking* about it."

"If you do vote for Mondale, will you tell your friends?" Brian asked.

"Sometimes it's just classier to keep opinions to yourself," Franklin said.

"Better to be dead than rude, is that your position?" I suggested.

That was a bit too far for Joseph's taste. "I think we should put a moratorium on politics until after the election." He followed that up with a dirty look for me.

Toward the end of dinner, I realized that Brian didn't talk as much about his volunteer work at Howard Brown. I guessed that he probably wasn't spending as much time there since Ross came back. He also didn't bring up the HTLV-III test that would be out soon. I was glad about that.

I didn't need a test to know who at the table probably had it and who didn't. Brian and I probably had it. We'd both had a lot of sex with people who we now knew had AIDS, not to mention each other. Franklin and Joseph were fine. Well, Joseph was fine since he hadn't started having sex until after we knew about condoms. Franklin acted like he was sure he didn't have it, but that might not mean anything.

After everyone left, Joseph cornered me in the bedroom and said, "You need to be nicer to Franklin. He's not going anywhere."

"I like Franklin better than I like his friends."

"He'll choose Brian over his friends. He just hasn't done it yet."

Normally, I would have walked out to the street and hailed a cab, but the suitcase Brian lent me had gotten remarkably heavy. If I didn't think I needed something, Joseph thought I did, so I ended up with far more than I needed. Rather than walk a block and end up with my right arm stretched out like an old elastic waistband, I called Flash Cab. The driver arrived quickly and got me to the airport in about thirty-five minutes.

Fully one-third of O'Hare was a construction site. I could see that even though we were on the second level. I'd read something in the *Daily Herald* about the expansion they'd been planning, I just hadn't known it was underway. My cab pulled up in front of Terminal 2, which was basically a large glass box held together by strips of black metal. I paid the driver almost twenty bucks and pushed my suitcase out of the passenger side following after it.

Even at midnight, there were people wandering around. I suspected it was much busier in the daytime. I walked into the terminal and right in front of me, on the other side, was a large open space with the check-in desks. My flight was on Frontier. I had to walk halfway down the terminal to find the Frontier desks. There were only three of them.

My stomach was doing calisthenics as I stood there holding tight to Brian's over-stuffed suitcase. One of the desks was open so I walked over. Behind the desk was a pretty young woman who'd made a half-hearted attempted to push a mass of curls under a baseball cap with the red-and-white Frontier logo on the front. She wore a red uniform that matched the logo as well, and had a white kerchief around her neck.

"Hi, I'm on the flight to Las Vegas."

"Ticket?"

"Oh, sure," I said. I set the suitcase on the floor and reached into my inside lapel pocket to get the envelope that had been sent over by Cooke, Babcock and Lackerby. Inside were my itinerary, hotel reservations, rental car reservations, airline ticket and the five hundred dollars in cash. The ticket had a thin cover sheet featuring the

Frontier logo over two cardstock tickets: one going and one returning. I handed the whole thing over to the clerk and she studied the first ticket.

"You have a bag?

She couldn't see it? It was baby blue. "Yes, right here."

"Put it on the scale please."

I did. She glanced quickly at my bag and sighed. "Here. Fill this out." She handed me a label with a bit of string on the end. Then she shoved a pen my way. Quickly, I filled out my name and address.

Meanwhile, she typed into a CRT. I could hear a printer clacking away under the desk. She pulled out another card stock strip and tucked it together with my return ticket. "Here's your boarding pass and baggage claim."

"Thanks." I offered her the label I made out.

"Put it on your luggage please."

"Oh. All right."

God, it was so obvious I'd never done this before. She put a tag on my suitcase that had LAS printed on it. I looped the luggage label around the handle next to the tag. She must have taken pity on me because she said, "Your gate is E10." She pointed back the way I'd come. "Just follow the signs. Flight 145."

"Thank you," I said, reaching for my suitcase.

"No. I keep that." Then, with a heave, she picked up the suitcase and put it on a conveyor belt behind her. Awkwardly, I walked away.

To actually enter the terminal, I had to go through a metal detector almost exactly like the one I'd been walking through every day at the courthouse. I threw my keys in a plastic dish that reminded me of the pans they give you to vomit in when you're in the hospital and then walked through without a problem. Got my keys back and headed out to Concourse E.

Over dinner, there had been a long discussion as to whether I'd be able to sleep on the plane. Franklin said that the vibration would put me to sleep, but Brian never slept on airplanes and apologized for not bringing me a Valium. That earned him a sidelong glance from Franklin who apparently didn't have the good sense to go through his boyfriend's medicine cabinet.

You'd think after that discussion I'd have remembered to bring *Fatal Vision* so I could it finish it on the flight. But I hadn't. I stopped at a newsstand and picked up *People*, *Time* and the *Tribune*—since I'd read the *Daily Herald* that morning. I could have picked up a paperback—Orwell's *1984* was prominently featured on the spinning rack of books—but I wasn't sure I could focus on much more than gossip and watered down politics.

There weren't a lot of people at my gate. Most of the gates were nearly empty. There were people wandering here and there, but the only crowd I saw on the concourse was in a small, dark bar with the ridiculous name Shipyard. I sat down in a narrow seat covered in baby blue vinyl and attached to a metal bar.

The *Tribune's* front-page story was about how Reagan's tax cuts weren't really working out for anyone who didn't have a tax accountant. Despite the fact that he was campaigning on how he'd cut everyone's taxes, apparently he hadn't actually done that. Not that anyone would figure out it was Reagan's fault. That seemed to support the things that Brian was saying. Still, people were reluctant to blame Reagan for anything; he seemed like too nice a guy to actually hurt them.

I tried to keep focused on the article but instead took my Swatch out of my pocket and checked the time. I had nearly an hour so I walked back down to the Shipyard, squeezed my way up to the bar, and after a minute or so got the bartender's attention to order a Johnnie Walker Red on the rocks.

I'd barely taken a sip of my drink, when I noticed a short man with sun-bleached hair, and overly tanned skin looking at me intently. He noticed me noticing him and moved down the bar to stand next to me. He wore a peach-colored polo shirt and madras shorts. Shorts. In Chicago. In October.

"Where are you heading?" he asked.

"Las Vegas."

"Me too! Isn't that a coincidence?" It probably wasn't. I had the feeling half the people in the bar, mostly men, were waiting on gate E10.

"Do you like to gamble?" he asked.

"Every day." Well, I took chances.

"Me too! I play the lottery wherever I am. Love it. I've been here three days. I played the Daily Game each day and the Pick 4 twice. I won a hundred and fifty bucks yesterday. I'm lucky like that. Did you hear about that guy last month, though? Forty million! Oh my God, what I could do with forty million dollars, you know?"

"So you're going to Las Vegas to gamble?"

"Yes. And no. I'm going on business, but I'll definitely spend some time at that tables. I'm in sales. I sell sitcoms to independent TV stations. Syndication. I was here for a big meeting at WGN. I'm meeting with KVVU first thing Monday. Busy life, you know?"

"So you live in Hollywood?"

"Oh, God no. I live in Santa Monica. Only dopers and wannabe actors live in Hollywood. You don't know anything about L.A., do you?"

"Nope."

"No one does. Even the people who live there. Can I buy you a drink?"

"I've barely started this one. But thanks."

"You married?"

"No."

"That's so smart. I love my wife, I love my kids, but damn it's like I'm on a treadmill and it's never gonna stop, you know? I mean, the mortgage, the private schools, the cars, and Jesus Christ, the vacations. Every time I have even a couple of days off the wife wants to go somewhere. I mean, it's like she hasn't noticed that I travel for a living and maybe I'd like to actually see the house I'm paying for before we run off to Hawaii or Puerto Vallarta. What seat did you get?"

I hadn't even looked. I pulled the boarding pass out of my inside jacket pocket and saw that I was in 6C. I told the guy where my seat was. Not that I thought it was a good idea.

"That's an aisle seat. Good for you. You're tall. You can stretch your legs. I like the window seat; like to know what's going on. And I'm vertically challenged, so I don't get cramped like you would. I'm in 14F. Can you believe there's no first class on this flight? I'm calling our travel department on Monday to complain. You play golf?"

"No."

"Lucky you. I *hate* golf. But I have to play it all the time. These station managers, they're crazy for golf. They could give a shit about TV shows and movies, it's all widgets to them, but golf they go nuts for."

"No kidding," I said. I don't know why I bothered though, I didn't think it mattered to this guy whether I contributed to the conversation or not.

"What's your name? I'm Wes Bollen."

"Nick. Nick Nowak."

"What do you do for a living, Nick?"

"I work for a law office. I'm going down to Las Vegas to pick up some documents."

"Really? Must be important documents if they can't FedEx them."

"I really can't say." Just because I was lying was no reason to breach confidentiality.

"So, you're not a lawyer, are you?" Wes asked, but I could barely hear him. A woman's voice came over a loudspeaker. All I really heard were tiny bits of what she was saying. But the words "Vegas" and "boarding" were enough to get me to finish my drink.

"They just called our flight, didn't they?"

"Oh yeah. But we've still got thirty-five minutes. Let me buy you another drink."

"No. That's fine. I just wanna get on the plane." I also wanted to never get on the plane, but since I had to fly to Las Vegas, I had no choice. Might as well get the show on the road.

"Anxious, are we? You know, prostitution is legal in Nevada. That's probably why you're in such a rush."

"What can I say? You got me."

Chapter Ten

If there is such a place as hell it will feature experiences similar to boarding an airplane. While there were only about forty of us, it still seemed to take forever to get everything sorted out and all of us onto the plane. Getting on, the first thing I noticed was that it wouldn't be even half full. There were about a hundred and fifty seats. I also had the terrible realization the airplane wasn't much bigger than a CTA bus. I kept thinking, "I'm on a fucking bus with wings."

I didn't like that. Didn't like it at all.

After I found my seat, I decided to distract myself by making a mental list of things I needed to do once I got to Las Vegas. It would be around 7 a.m. I had to rent a car, get a map of the city, check into Lucky Days, find out where the county jail was—hopefully, it was actually in Las Vegas, though it could be anywhere in the county. Mickey had been staying at the hotel, so I should show his picture around and find out what I could about his stay. Reflexively, I slipped a hand into my jacket pocket to find that the photo I'd stolen from his parents' house was still there.

Wes Bollen came down the aisle and nodded to me on the way to his seat. I nodded back. There were three gray cloth seats on either side of the plane. A woman just a few years younger than Mrs. Harker sat by the window on my side of the plane. A young cuddling couple took up most of the three seats across from me. Other than that, the seats were tall enough that it was a challenge to see much beyond the tops of people's heads.

I opened *People* and had to decide whether to look at the first pictures of Prince Harry, read up on the stunningly gorgeous TV actor who'd managed to kill himself by firing a blank at his head, or the story of a boy who spent his entire life in a plastic bubble. None of that really drew my attention, so I switched over to *Time*. Much of the issue was devoted to politics. I liked reading about politics. It had so little to do with real life. I was absorbed by the pressing questions "Was Reagan too old?" and would Americans ever elect a woman to the presidency, while the two stewardesses and one steward managed to get everyone seated and accounted for.

Then with a disturbing lurch, the airplane began to back up and we were on our way. The next twenty minutes were among the most terrifying of my life, which is saying something since I've been stabbed twice, hit with a baseball bat, beaten, strangled, and dropped onto a moving El train. What made our ascent so terrifying was my absolute lack of control—even tied naked to a chair I could plan an escape—and everyone else's complacency. While chugging like the "Little Engine That Could," the airplane rose at an angle so disturbing I worried we might flip over backward. Then, there were these terrible pauses when the engine would seem to stop, making the airplane slow down and pitch forward, leaving me wondering if jet engines were supposed to do that or had they possibly malfunctioned.

Finally, we took on a relatively level position and the no-smoking lights turned off. Thank God. I immediately flipped up the postage stamp sized ashtray in the arm of my seat and lit a cigarette. Just as immediately, the woman next to me reached up and pressed a button on the console above us. I was barely halfway through my cigarette when the steward showed up at the end of my row.

"Sir, this is the no-smoking section." He was young, almost good-looking and frowning sternly. In fairness, the frowning might have been a reaction to his having to wear a polyester uniform of red pants and a red vest.

"There's an ashtray," I pointed out.

"Yes, well this is an old plane." That did not lessen my need to smoke.

"Where is the smoking section?"

"It's in the back. There are plenty of seats if you'd like to move."

"You want me to go to the back of the bus?"

"It's an airplane, sir. And it's not a racial thing."

I stacked my magazines and newspaper, undid my seatbelt and, after the steward stepped out of my way, walked to the very back of the airplane. There were only about six people back there. All of whom were smoking. I claimed a seat in a completely empty row. I don't know why, but the idea of plummeting back to earth was more appealing if I had a bit of privacy. I put out my cigarette and immediately lit another.

A half an hour later I felt almost normal. The two stewardesses had come by with a drink cart and I was able to purchase three tiny bottles of Johnnie Walker Red. I poured two bottles into the tiny plastic glass they'd filled with ice for me. Then took a large enough first gulp that I could fit in the third bottle.

I was trying very hard to be reasonable. Airplanes flew every day, every hour, possibly every minute. Very few of them crashed. My fears were completely ridiculous. But, in the event they weren't, I would not be dying sober or nicotine-free.

I'd managed to down most of the scotch when I looked up to find Wes Bollen standing next to me in the aisle.

"Let me in," he said.

I picked up my drink, lifted up the tray table, and scooted back a bit. Wes crawled over me, pushed aside the blanket and the pillows that were left out on the seats and flipped up the arm, allowing him to sprawl over the two other seats in my row.

"What can I do for you?" I asked.

"Everyone around me was snoring."

As soon as they'd finished with the drink cart they'd turned the lights down low.

"You know, I've been flying a long time," he continued. "There used to be an airline that had the stewardesses decked out in hot pants. Those were the days."

"Uh-huh," I said. I wasn't interested in sexy stewardesses, nor was I interested in explaining why.

"Do you want to join the mile high club?" he asked.

For the briefest moment, I thought he was talking about some kind of airline frequent flier club. Then I got it. He'd been saying things about women to gauge my reaction. Since it was pretty nonexistent...

"Oh. Um..."

It *was* Friday and he wasn't unattractive. Or at least he'd look better without his wacky shorts. Still, there was an immediate question that came to mind. Where? Where exactly were we going to do it? Wes answered that before I could ask by taking a blanket out of its plastic wrap and spreading it across my lap. Very quickly his hands were under the blanket undoing my jeans.

"You look surprised," Wes said. "Look, I love my wife but she doesn't have a dick, you know?"

"Yeah, that would have been my guess." I also guessed he said "I love my wife but…" a lot.

"I'm bisexual. Like Elton John."

"A lot of people are," I said. Wes was hardly the first guy I'd had sex with who thought of himself as bisexual. For some reason, that type made a beeline for me. "What does your wife do while you're off being bisexual?"

His hand was inside my boxers, pulling on my dick, making it hard. With a shrug, he said, "I think she enjoys the fact that I'm not bothering her. She's not very interested in sex."

"Pity."

"You adapt." He leaned a bit closer and said, "You have a really nice dick. It has girth." He managed to make the word girth sound incredibly obscene. "It's too good to pass up. I'm going to the restroom. I'll leave the door unlocked. Wait thirty seconds and follow me."

Then he climbed over me and went back to the restroom, two rows behind me. I finished the rest of my scotch. I have to say, my attitude about flying had begun to improve.

When the thirty seconds were up, I adjusted myself so that I could stand and walked back toward the restroom. The steward stood in the galley behind the restrooms with his arms crossed. As I opened the door to follow Wes he raised a judgmental eyebrow.

The restroom was incredibly small. Wes and I were pressed together. That was the plan, but it was also the only option. He reached over me and slid the lock.

"I think the steward knows exactly what we're doing," I said.

"In that case, we'd better hurry." He turned around, pulled down his loud shorts, and leaned over, bracing himself on the curving cabin wall. I looked down and there was his very white, very creamy ass. A crisp, brown tan-line ran across the bit of his back that I could see.

"Do you have a condom?" I asked.

"A what? Are you kidding? Do you think I'm not clean? I am very hygienic down there."

"It's an AIDS thing. You don't get AIDS if you use a condom."

"No kidding? Well, I can't go around with condoms. My wife's on the pill. If she found them she'd think I was fucking whores."

"Well, I don't have one." On me. I had plenty in my suitcase down in the luggage hold. It hadn't occurred to me that I might need one on the flight.

"Does that mean you're not going to fuck me?"

"I guess not. Sorry."

"Whatever."

I thought he might push me out of the way and go back to his seat. Instead, he knocked me up against the door and squeezed himself onto the tiny square of floor. Deftly, he undid my 501s, pulling them and my boxers down to my knees. He had my dick deep in the back of his throat and was tickling my balls in a matter of seconds.

I was fuzzy on how safe it was to do this without a condom. I mean, Brian would probably say it was necessary, but I hadn't been using one with Joseph; we agreed that it had all the appeal of sucking on a plastic bag, because you *were* basically sucking on a plastic bag. Our compromise was using lots of mouthwash and not coming in each other's mouths. This didn't seem an appropriate time to discuss the issue with Wes, though.

He stopped what he was doing. Holding my half hard dick in his hand he looked up at me and said, "Whatever you're thinking about, stop. Thinking and hard dicks don't go together."

I couldn't say he was wrong, so I took his advice and closed my eyes. I emptied my mind, tried to think of nothing but the way his tongue was teasing the end of my cock. As I relaxed, my dick got harder. Wes took a break and used his hand to jerk me a few times. I glanced down and saw his hard, red dick bobbing around my ankles.

He dove back down on me and I dug my hands into his hair. I guided him up and down. Then, just a minute or so later, close to coming, I pulled him off me, reached down and started jacking myself. Seeing that I was close, Wes held his mouth wide open so he could catch my cum.

I twisted his head to one side and angled my dick so that when I came I sprayed him all over his neck. Turned out there wasn't much point to that since he immediately used two fingers to scrape the cum off his throat and pop it into his mouth. I decided to skip the long discussion on why that might not be a good idea.

As I pulled up my shorts, I noticed that his prick was still hard as nails and throbbing. "Do you want a hand with that?"

He shook his head. "What about that steward? Do you think he'll fuck me?"

"Maybe if you ask nicely."

Landing was less stressful than taking off. The plane gradually eased downward over a long distance, suggesting to me that the pilot might have some actual skill. The desert was still pitch black, not surprising at nearly 5:30

a.m., I guess. But wait, that was the time in Chicago. It was after seven in Las Vegas. I needed to reset the watch for the two-hour time difference. I just hadn't bothered. The sun should be up, though. Shouldn't it?

Toward the end of the flight, I'd gotten maybe twenty minutes of real sleep and maybe an hour of semi-drowsing. I was awake long enough to notice Wes returning to the restroom three times. I'm guessing one of those times he actually took a piss.

Being in the back of the plane, I had to wait until just about everyone else had gotten off. I deplaned, as they say, walking by the steward who was saying goodbye to everyone.

"I hope you enjoyed your flight," he said to me in a pointed way.

"And I hope you enjoyed yours, too."

After walking down a kind of portable hallway, I found myself in a circular terminal. People had scattered around when I got to the gate; a family was greeting their grown son, a girl meeting a possible boyfriend or brother. Most of my flight went unmet.

I wasn't too far from the gate when I encountered the first row of slot machines. Lights were flashing, the machines were beeping, but no one was playing them. In fact, the whole airport had a weird sense of calm about it. Like it was the middle of the night instead of moments before dawn. The janitors were still buffing the floor.

Following the signs to baggage claim, I ended up waiting at a conveyor belt on the ground floor. As I waited, I stared out the large glass window. Across the street, they were building something, something big. I guess that's what Ronnie was doing with the money he squeezed out of waiters and other low-wage earners: He was building airports.

It took me a minute to realize there was something wrong with the construction site. There were no workers. I figured it was getting close to eight by then; wouldn't a crew have started? I looked around for a clock but didn't see one. Nothing was happening with the baggage, so I wandered over to a bank of TV screens hung on up in the air. Computers somewhere put up the flight times. I scanned them looking for my flight. FRNT 145 arrived at three fifty. Shit. I'd fucked up the time difference. I'd added instead of subtracting.

Taking another look at the Swatch, it showed it was now six ten in Chicago, so it was 4 a.m. in Las Vegas. Great. What would I do until the Alamo counter opened? And when would it open? I went back to baggage claim. Nothing was happening.

I recognized the people from my flight. They all looked exhausted, even Wes who looked exhausted *and* sated. I imagined the baggage handlers fast asleep in the back while our luggage sat there. Eventually, the conveyor belt started and luggage began coming out one lonely piece at a time. I sidled over to Wes and asked, "Hey, when do the rental car places open?"

"They never close. This is the city that never sleeps."

I was pretty sure that was New York, but I didn't argue. Even without leaving the airport I suspected Las Vegas might have a bad case of insomnia. Brian's baby blue suitcase came through the rubber flaps, so I grabbed it, nodded a goodbye to Wes, and began making my way to the Alamo counter.

The nice thing was that everything was handled by Cooke, Babcock and Lackerby. The not very nice thing was that—after I turned in my paperwork at the Alamo desk and was handed off to a very drowsy, very old black man who drove me to a nearly empty parking lot—I was given a brand new 1985 maroon Pontiac 1000.

A Pontiac 1000 is the car you buy if you want a Chevy Chevette but are too embarrassed to say so. In fact, other than the logos, it looked exactly like a Chevette. Boxy with smoothed off edges and oh so dull. I unlocked the hatchback and put my suitcase in the quasi-trunk. Then I went around and got into the driver's seat – the red-and-beige plaid driver's seat. I did my best to adjust the seat. Unfortunately, my options were driving with my head jammed against the roof of the car or putting the seat nearly all the way back and adopting a semi-prone position. I went with the second.

I'd picked up a map of the city at the rental desk, so the first thing I did was open it up on the steering wheel and plot my course to Lucky Days. The casino was at Sahara Boulevard and South Las Vegas Boulevard. All I had to do was find my way out of the rental parking lot to Tropicana Avenue, head west until I got to Las Vegas Boulevard and then go north. I wasn't entirely sure which way was north, so I focused on taking a left, then a right.

The lights from the casino cast a glow against the night sky so in the end, it wasn't hard to figure out where I was going. At the intersection, the famous Tropicana with its name in vertical neon on one whole side of the building was on my left. The Marina Hotel and Casino sat on my right. It was a fifteen-story hotel with a circular water logo and an enormous sign that told you Jerry Van Dyke was playing in the Mirage Room. On the other side of the street a dusty empty lot on one side and a gas station on the other.

Las Vegas Boulevard was wide, three whole lanes on each side with a gravel median in the middle. I rolled down the window. It wasn't hot like I thought the desert would be. In fact, it was a bit chilly, but the car was claustrophobic and the cool air felt good. I passed by several other gas stations: Texaco, Chevron, Shell. And then a half-dozen motels before I got to Aladdin and then The Jockey Club. I had the feeling this was not a very happening part of town. Or at least I hoped that was the case.

I passed by the MGM Grand on my right with its Aztec pyramid-shaped casino squatting in front of the mid-rise hotel. I remembered they'd had a deadly fire just a few years before. It had all seemed so big on the front page of *The Daily Herald*, but felt much smaller in person.

The next intersection was Dunes-Flamingo and then there were a lot more casinos. Famous ones. Caesars Palace, the Flamingo, the Sands, Castaways. Their signs boasted entertainers like Rich Little, Paul Anka, Lola Falana and Liberace. Siegfried and Roy were at Frontier— Joseph and I had watched a repeat of *Lifestyles of the Rich and Famous* showing them at home. Together. They had to be the most famous gay couple in America who couldn't say they were gay or a couple.

After that, I arrived at Sahara Boulevard. On my right, I could see the Lucky Days sign. It was done in bold, sprawling cursive and bright green neon. The sign below bragged that magician Kip Callahan was in the Fortune Forum and Gary Glenn's *Les Femmes* was in the Kismet Room. They also had a breakfast buffet for $2.95.

The hotel itself was a rectangular slab probably twenty stories tall, faced in shimmering Kelly green glass with the top floor set back so that each penthouse suite had a balcony. Next to the hotel was a two-story building covering several acres—which I'd find out later was the casino, a three-story parking garage and, in front of it all, a fanning awning lined in flashing gold lights that covered the entrance.

I pulled in and stopped in front of a teenaged valet wearing a green-and-gold jacket who looked like he was at the end of his shift. When I asked about guest parking he looked relieved. He wouldn't have to lower himself to park my cheesy little rental.

"The parking structure is in the back of the building. You have to go out to Las Vegas Boulevard, take a right down to St. Louie, and then take another right on Paradise and a third right at Sahara." I must have looked a little confused because he added, "Basically you're going round the block. A pain in the ass, I know. We have to do it all the time."

I started to ask why I couldn't go the other way, then I realized the median running down the center of Las Vegas Boulevard had changed to concrete. Which sucked. I nodded my thanks and then drove out onto the boulevard again. After making the required three rights, I was able to pull into the concrete parking garage behind the hotel.

The first floor had a prominent sign that said, VALET PARKING ONLY. That was not even half full, meaning a lot of people did the right-right-right thing. As soon as valet parking ended and guest parking began, every single space was taken. I found a spot on the third floor about as far from the elevator as you could get and decided to be grateful. As near as I could tell there were only three spaces to choose from. I grabbed my suitcase out of the back and walked across the garage. It was a lovely place, decorated in soot and cigarette butts.

The elevator dumped me into the casino, which I had to cross to get to the reservations desk. The carpet was green and gold. The slot machines clinked and clanged even when no one was near them. In the center of the casino was an area devoted to table games; blackjack, craps, roulette. There were about twenty tables, but only two of them had players. Of course, it was still well before breakfast. Speaking of which, I was starving. I decided that as soon as I dumped my suitcase in my room I'd find the breakfast buffet and relieve myself of three bucks.

The registration desk was about forty feet of green marble and had ten CRT stations. At five-thirty in the morning though there was only one clerk and no line. I walked up to her. She was about forty and looked like she had a bad hangover.

"Good morning. I have a reservation."

"Name please."

"Nick Nowak."

She could have said welcome to Lucky Days or good morning or even hello. Instead, she clicked my name into her computer monitor and chewed her tongue while she waited for my reservation to appear. It must have appeared because she said, "I need a driver's license and a credit card."

I pulled out my wallet and handed her my license.

"Why do you need my credit card? This is taken care of."

"Incidentals. Not everything you charge to your room will be covered by..." She squinted at the screen. "Babcock, Cooke and Lake-bee."

"Lackerby."

Without reacting, she looked down at my license, then up at me. She offered it back to me. Unhappily, I handed her my credit card. I wasn't planning on charging much of anything to the room. A meal maybe. Some phone calls.

She ran my credit card through an imprinter and then handed it back to me with the slip for me to sign. I wasn't too happy about signing a blank credit card slip but I figured Jimmy would take care of any problems.

"You've got early check-in. Normally, you can't check-in until afternoon."

I guess I was supposed to feel special.

I put my credit card and the carbon she gave me into my pocket right next to Mickey's photo. *Well*, I thought, *might as well get to work*. The clerk had kept busy by making a few notations on her computer and then sending something to the communal printer. When she came back to me, she ripped the perforations off a sheet and said, "Sign at the bottom please."

Before I did I slipped the photo of Mickey across the desk. "Do you know this guy?"

She picked up the photo and glanced at it. Though why she bothered, I don't know.

"I can't comment on other guests," she said.

"He's the reason—"

"And even if I could, there are fourteen desk clerks working at Lucky Days. We have almost four hundred rooms. Even if I did check him in or check him out, I don't think I'd remember him. The only people I remember are the ones who cause problems." She gave me a look that said, "I'll be remembering you."

"He was here for almost seven weeks. The law firm I work for represents Jimmy English."

She gave me a hard look. "I'm not bullshitting you. I don't know the guy. My shift is from seven to four. That means mostly I do check-outs. You have an early check-in. That means we charge the law firm you work for an extra day. Our average guests try to avoid that fee. It's possible the guy checked in and out without ever seeing me."

"All right. If he was here for seven weeks, who would he have seen?"

"They might know him at the concierge desk. They arrange show tickets, dinner reservations, golf outings, things of that sort. There are also three restaurants and two bars in the hotel. He might be known at any of those places. And if he's a big roller they'll know him in the pits."

"Thanks. I appreciate it. You've been helpful."

She didn't seem to appreciate the thanks. Instead, she slid a set of keys my way. Two keys, each attached to a disgusting rabbit's foot.

"Look, I know the kind of people I work for so I shouldn't say this but... I hope you're not here to kill the poor guy."

"No. I think I'm here to save him."

Chapter Eleven

It had been about a decade since shag haircuts were popular, but three of the four waitresses at the Wishbone Inn wore the style, making them all look distantly related to Florence Henderson. I'd dumped my bag off in my room, 1614, which luckily turned out not to be green. If it had been green I might have thrown something through the hermetically sealed window and jumped.

Although I was pretty exhausted, I'd had nothing but a couple of bags of peanuts for the last thirteen hours, so I decided to have breakfast before I passed out for a few hours. Since I was there to do more than eat and sleep, I thought I'd pass Mickey's picture around at the breakfast buffet, take a nap, and then do the same at lunch. My plan for the afternoon was to find the county jail and make sure Mickey wasn't tucked away there.

When it came down to it, there wasn't a lot to waiting on people at a buffet. My waitress was named Fernie and she came right over when I sat down. Without asking, she picked up the coffee cup that was already there and filled it to the brim with thick, dark coffee.

"You wanna Keno card?"

"What?" I asked.

"A Keno card. You buy a card from me and you can play while you have breakfast." She tipped her head toward a board with numbers that lighted up. "It's like bingo but you don't have to shout if you win."

"Thanks, I'll just have breakfast."

"Sure. You can help yourself whenever you're ready. Plates are at that end." She waved vaguely in the direction of the long buffet. "Carlos will make you an omelet if you want. If he's not standing there at the end, just holler."

"I got it. Don't shout for Keno. Shout for an omelet."

That got me a faded smile. She turned to walk away.

"Hold on a second." I dug around in my jacket and found the picture of Mickey. I laid it on the table with a five-dollar bill. Not a bad tip on a three-dollar buffet. "Have you seen this guy?"

She picked up the picture and looked at it closely. "Yeah. He's been in here."

"Can you tell me anything about him? Who he was with? How he looked? Anything?"

"Can I show this to the other girls?"

"Sure. Just make sure I get it back."

Blandly, she snatched up the five spot and walked away. I went over to the buffet. It wasn't what you'd call gourmet, but it was plentiful. I stacked my plate with two blueberry muffins, three scoops of scrambled eggs, a half a pound of bacon, grits, sausage gravy, two waffles with a pint of syrup—and a side dish of fruit, because I like to eat healthy. I was back at my table and halfway through my breakfast when Fernie came back. She set the picture onto the table.

"Most of the girls saw him. Couple times he was in with one of them girls from *Les Femmes*. Tiny little thing, real pretty."

"How did you know she was a showgirl? Not every pretty girl in Vegas is a showgirl, right?"

She didn't seem to like my attitude. Didn't want to be challenged. "Yeah, you're right some of them's hookers."

"So maybe she was a hooker?"

"Naw, she was one of them girls. She's the one on the billboard."

"What billboard?"

"For *Les Femmes*. It's all over town."

"Ah, I just got here a couple hours ago."

"Yeah. Well, have a nice stay."

"They only came in for breakfast? The guy I'm looking for and the showgirl."

"All the girls here right now work the breakfast/lunch shift. You wanna know about dinner then you gotta come back later."

"Thanks."

Fernie wandered off and I worked on wolfing down the rest of my breakfast. Mickey had been at The Wishbone Inn a couple of times for breakfast with a showgirl. Sounded like he had a girlfriend. That didn't surprise me since I semi-remembered him saying he wanted to get married someday. Or maybe I didn't remember that. Maybe I remembered that he didn't like to think he was gay and I assumed that meant he'd want to get married. At the very least, it meant he was pretending an interest in girls. Showgirls. One showgirl.

Now I just needed to find her.

If you've ever seen a drag queen after a hard night, mascara running, makeup smudged, wig askew; that's Las Vegas in bright light. The neon signs are unimpressive, the empty lots as noticeable as missing teeth, the palm trees scraggly and lonely, the hotels large and looming, sprouting out of the desert like a poorly planned garden. I'm not sure what I was expecting Las Vegas to be like. Maybe more like the Loop with enormous buildings crammed together, one crazy thing to look at after another, people everywhere. At one in the afternoon, Las Vegas was barren and decidedly unglamorous.

I'd woken at twelve-thirty and decided that the giant lump in my stomach meant that I wasn't hungry. I pulled out the phone book from the nightstand next to the king-sized bed and flipped to Las Vegas Jail. There were several phone numbers: a general number, a number for juvenile arrests, and a number for prisoner lookup. I could simply call and ask if Mickey Troccoli was in residence. I didn't bother, though. If he was in the Las Vegas Jail he wasn't there under his real name. I needed to go down and find someone who might recognize him.

I took a quick shower and put on a white oxford shirt that had wrinkled badly in my suitcase. There was an iron in the room, but I hadn't been sent to Las Vegas to iron shirts so I didn't bother. When I located my rental car again, I unfolded the map and picked out where I was going. Basically, it was down the street just past what the map called DOWNTOWN. It took me a whole fifteen minutes to get there and five of that was spent finding my way out of the parking structure and back to Las Vegas Boulevard.

Las Vegas City Hall was an ultra mod building that looked like a couple of beige wheels of cheese sitting on top of each other. Someone had taken a healthy chunk of cheese off one side. Maybe they used it to make the parking structure. As I pulled in, I couldn't help noticing that the cheesy motel across the street had a big sign that said, "Elvis Slept Here." I was tempted to make my own sign and stand underneath theirs. Mine would say, "Why?"

The jail was on the second floor and wasn't especially hard to find. I didn't go up though. By the time I got to the first floor, I wondered if I wasn't wasting my time. I knew what I was about to encounter. I'd go up to the jail, ask around until I found some bored, possibly disgruntled city worker who would tell me there was no Michelangelo Troccoli in residence. I'd show them the picture and they'd shrug. At the end of the day, I'd have no real idea if Mickey was in there or not. I had to find another way to figure this out.

I hung out in a kind of atrium for a while, smoking a cigarette and trying to figure out where I was. City Hall. The mayor's offices were here somewhere. The city council. Did they have aldermen in Las Vegas? I had no idea. Important people, though, worked in this building. Right on top of the city jail. So, did the mayor come to work every day and ride the elevator with vagrants who'd been picked up drunk in front of the casinos? Somehow I didn't think so. There had to be an entrance where they brought the prisoners in and where they let them out. And it didn't face onto the pretty atrium.

Going back out to the street, I meant to walk around the entire building but stopped when I got around the corner. There was a door opening onto to the sidewalk. Next to the door was a plaque with the major's name and four councilmen below that. This was their private entrance. So the pretty atrium *was* actually for the riff-raff.

Returning to the atrium, I hung out next to a trashcan that had an ashtray stuck on the top. New Year's was two months off and I should probably give some thought to quitting smoking. Again. Of course, every time I thought about quitting smoking I wanted a cigarette, sort of defeating the whole purpose. I smoked and watched people come in and out. I was looking for something. I just wasn't sure what.

Sooner or later I would have to get another pack of cigarettes. That's what I was thinking about when I noticed a woman in her late thirties with a boy who was in his early twenties. I caught a snippet of what he was saying "…in there for four days…"

To which the woman responded, "Today is payday. How could I get you out before payday?"

I stubbed out my cigarette and went after them. "Excuse me, did you just get out of jail?"

The boy said, "Fuck off."

"Look, I'm harmless. I think my brother's in there but he's using another name. Can you just look at his picture? I'll give you twenty bucks."

That stopped the boy. The woman, who I realized was his very young mother, frowned. She didn't seem happy that I was giving him money. My guess was he'd been picked up on a drug or alcohol charge. She'd deliberately left him to cool his heels and sober up. Now, I was giving him the means to get wasted again.

I showed him the picture of Mickey. He shook his head and held out his hand for the money, "No. I didn't see him in there."

"Does the jail have cells or is it more like a dormitory?"

"Cells."

"But they grouped you together for meals, right?"

"And exercise."

"So if he was in there you'd have seen him?"

"Yeah. But I said I didn't."

"You didn't hear anything about a prisoner they were keeping separate."

"No." He gave me an annoyed look. "But if you want me to say yes, I will. Whatever it takes to get the twenty bucks."

I reached into my pocket.

"Don't give it to him," the mom said. "He'll just buy booze and drink himself back in here."

So it was booze, not drugs. Took longer but was just as effective. I offered the twenty to the mom.

"Hey!" the boy said. "What the fuck?"

"You owe your mom bail. Now you owe her twenty bucks less."

The woman smiled at me and then pulled her son away. I stood there for a few minutes chewing on what I'd found out. Mickey probably wasn't in there. So, that made it more likely that the ASA hadn't cut a deal to have him hidden. Yeah, they might have him somewhere else. This was a city facility. There was probably a county facility somewhere.

Suddenly, I realized I was going at this all wrong. I needed to get a quick picture of what Mickey had been up to since he got to Las Vegas. I particularly needed to know what was going on in his life around the time he left Lucky Days. If he was picked up by the police then, yeah, they might have him hidden somewhere. But there were also half a dozen other things that could have happened.

I went back to the rental and headed to Lucky Days. Except I didn't. I made a wrong turn and it took ten minutes of driving what turned out to be north for me to figure that out. In Chicago, I always kind of knew where the lake was and the lake was always to the east. Here there was nothing but a lot of dusty mountains every which way you looked.

Looking around, it was apparent that I'd stumbled onto the 'real' Las Vegas, the part people actually lived in.

Sun-bleached apartment buildings full of cocktail waitresses and blackjack dealers. Affordable senior living at the Peter Pan Motel. Boarded up storefronts of businesses that had failed. I started to get the idea that in the sixties and seventies the town was a sprawl of two story motels that did a healthy business. Then the big hotels started coming in, pulling all the customers.

I kept driving until I stumbled across Sahara Avenue and turned in what I hoped was a westerly direction. About two blocks down I saw the billboard. I pulled over to the side of the road a bit too quickly, earning me the finger from a guy in a white Chrysler Cordoba with a T-bar roof. I leaned over the steering wheel to get a better look. A lovely, young, blonde woman was sprawled across the sign in very little more than sequins. Hugging her curves were the words: Gary Glenn's *Les Femmes*. At the bottom of the billboard was the logo for Lucky Days. I took a good look at the woman's face, trying to remember it.

When I was pretty sure I'd remember it, I put my blinker on, ready to pull back into traffic. That's when I saw something across the way almost as interesting. On the other side of the street was a storefront, one that wasn't boarded up, in a one-story building with a big sign on top that read YE OLDE GUN SHOPPE. Underneath another sign, attached to the bigger one, said, NO WAIT GUN SALES. I could walk in there and buy a gun. That was tempting.

But then I asked myself what I needed a gun for. I wasn't going to be bringing Mickey back at gunpoint. I seriously doubted ASA Sanchez would be sending down any CPD thugs like Devlin. That kind of police work had already messed up her case. That left Doves and the Outfit guys I was pretty sure I'd seen in court. The guys who'd disappeared as soon as ASA Sanchez had said Mickey was in Las Vegas and that he was informing on another case. I hadn't seen them anywhere, but then I'd only been there a few hours. What would I do if I did see them? And if they got to Mickey first?

I made a U-turn and parked in front of Ye Olde Gun Shoppe, and in less than a half an hour purchased a semi-automatic Beretta Cheetah with a seven round magazine.

Chapter Twelve

When I got back to Lucky Days, I went up to my room, adjusted the holster I'd bought so that it fit the way I liked, and slipped in the black Cheetah so it lay under my arm flat against my chest. The clerk at Ye Olde Gun Shoppe had mentioned that in Nevada I should have a carry permit if I was going to use the holster I purchased. Of course, he waited until after I purchased it to say so.

"I'm not going to be here long," I said.

He shrugged like it didn't matter. "It's like a traffic ticket if you get caught. Fifty bucks."

Of course, it would be a bigger problem than a traffic ticket if I got caught with it back in Chicago, but he didn't need to know that. As a private investigator, I could still get a carry license, I'd found that much out. There were just a lot of hoops to jump through. I didn't like jumping through hoops.

"By the way, how do I travel with this? Or do I need to send it through the mail."

"I hear you're fine if you unload it and put it in your checked luggage. People only have problems if they try to bring weapons onto the plane with them. If you're police they'll let you, but I'm getting the impression you're not police."

"No. I'm not."

I didn't like the fact that he was getting curious about me so I changed the subject by pointing to a sign on the wall that said SHOTGUN WEDDINGS $95.

"Do you really aim a shotgun at people and marry them?"

"It's not loaded."

Yeah, that made it so much better.

In addition to the gun and the holster, I'd purchased everything I needed to do my first cleaning of the gun and a box of ammo. The room had a small, wooden table and a couple of not-very-comfortable chairs sitting in front of the floor-to-ceiling window. I spent nearly an hour cleaning the gun. Yes, it was right out of the box, but there are often filings inside the barrel of a new gun. The whole idea of having a gun again was disturbing enough without risking that it might blow up in my face. When I was done, I pulled my Swatch out and saw that it was nearly six o'clock in Chicago. That meant it was four in Las Vegas.

I sat on the bed and read the cardboard facing stuck to the push button desk phone on the nightstand. It told me how to get an outside line, that all calls would be charged to the room, and how to use a prepaid calling card. I got an outside line and dialed my home number. Joseph picked up on the second ring.

"I've been waiting for you to call all day," Joseph said when he picked up.

"Hello. How are you?"

"Why didn't you call this morning? I wanted to know you got there okay." There was a noise in the background. "We…we wanted to know that you got there okay."

"Well, if the plane had crashed it would be on the news."

"That's not how I want to find out something like that."

I decided not to point out that if the plane had crashed I wouldn't have been able to call him to let him know. "Okay. I'm sorry. I should have called earlier."

"No. I'm sorry. Certain people got me riled up," he said, loud enough for Ross to hear. "I know you're working. I shouldn't have said anything."

"It's okay. And tell Ross I say hello." He did and then we were silent for a moment. Shy. I said, "Are you all better?"

"Yeah, I'm all better."

I didn't ask what he was going to do that night. I didn't ask on Fridays. There wasn't a rule against telling each other what we did on Fridays; it's just something we didn't do. Of course, now there would be an entire weekend not to ask about.

"How is Ross?"

"He roasted a chicken for dinner."

"He's a magician." Given the size of my oven. "Did Brian come over?"

"No, he and Franklin are going to see *The Odd Couple*."

"The TV series?"

"It used to be a play. They're doing a female version at the Shubert with Sally Struthers and Rita Moreno."

"Which one is Tony Randall?"

"I don't know. I'll ask Brian tomorrow."

I hadn't even been gone a whole twenty-four hours and it was nice to talk to him. Nice to talk about things that didn't matter much.

"I miss you."

"I miss you, too. Don't make a habit of going away like this."

"This is the first time in thirty-six years. I don't think I will."

"We should go someplace together."

"How about a picnic on the Belmont Rocks?"

"I was thinking Hawaii. Or Florida."

"I can already tell that travel's not my thing."

"It might be more your thing if you were doing it with someone you like."

"Love."

"Love."

"I need to get back to work. I'll call you tomorrow." Actually, I was starting to get hungry again. I was going to eat and then get back to work.

"Nick, don't do that. This is costing a fortune and you'll be back in two days."

"I know, but what if I want to talk to you?"

"Only call if you *need* to talk to me."

"I need to talk to you. I always need to talk to you."

When I hung up, I changed my shirt, strapped on my gun again, covered it with my corduroy jacket, grabbed the *Time* magazine I hadn't finished on the plane and went downstairs to find a restaurant. When I got to the casino, I turned left and went back to the reservations desk. Across the lobby was the concierge desk. A prissy-looking man of about fifty stood behind the desk attempting to look busy.

I showed him my room key and asked, "Which of the restaurants is good?"

"They're all delicious, sir. You look like the kind of man who enjoys a good steak, though. Why not try the Horseshoe Lounge?"

I reached into my pocket and got the picture of Mickey. "Have you seen this guy around?"

He smiled. "I didn't think you cared about restaurants. There's a brochure in your room that describes them all quite well." Then he looked at the photo and frowned. "Who are you? Exactly?"

"Nick Nowak. I'm a private investigator working for Jimmy English. You can check that with the front desk if you want."

He paled. "We may have a problem then. This is Mickey Troccoli. Two guys came by this afternoon asking about him. They didn't have a picture, but they knew his name and what he looked like. They said *they* were working for Jimmy."

"Are they staying here?"

"They didn't say they were, no."

"You didn't check."

"No. I didn't—I mean, I never expected someone to say they worked for Jimmy if they didn't." The poor guy was shaking. He should have been more careful. He should have made sure they were staying at the hotel and whether they were paying for their rooms, which would have indicated it might be okay to give them information.

"What did you tell them?"

"That I'd seen Mickey. Quite a lot in fact. His room was comped. When a room is comped the shows are also comped. I arranged for him to see *Les Femmes* probably twenty or twenty-five times."

"Twenty-five times?"

"Yeah. Some nights he saw both shows."

"Have you arranged tickets for him in the last week?"

"No. I haven't seen him. The other guys asked that, too."

The other guys. They were a problem. And they were one step ahead of me. "Did you get the other guys tickets for the show?"

He shook his head.

"Mickey was seen with one of the showgirls. The girl on the billboard. Do they know that?"

"Um, well…"

"Do they or don't they?"

"That's not a girl on the billboard. That's Gary Glenn. He's a female impersonator."

"Oh." Well, that was an embarrassing thing to miss. Why hadn't I picked that up earlier? I ignored the blush filling my cheeks. "I need to talk to Gary Glenn. How would I do that?"

"The show plays at nine and eleven. If you meet me here at ten fifteen I'll take you backstage."

"Great. I'll be here. In the meantime, do me a favor— check me out, make sure I'm who I say I am." I gave him my card so he'd remember my name.

"Sure, I can do that."

"And tell me, which way is the Horseshoe Lounge?"

The steak dinner I had wasn't half bad, but the three and half hours of sleep I got was better. When the front desk called me, I took a quick shower using the world's smallest bar of soap and was ready to go back downstairs by ten. I sat for a few minutes smoking and coming up with a plan. Gary Glenn was going to lead me to Mickey. The minute I got my hands on him I should drag him by the hair to the airport and get on the next flight to Chicago. I went ahead and packed since I might be leaving in a hurry.

When I got down to the concierge desk, the guy I'd spoken to earlier was standing there in his civilian clothes: jeans, a striped sweater and a maroon Members Only jacket.

"Is it cold out?" I asked. He seemed overdressed.

"It's the desert. It gets cold at night pretty fast." He nodded back toward the casino. "It's this way."

We started walking across the casino. As we walked by the gaming tables, I noticed that half of them were now full. Among the gamblers, I noticed several older women with mink coats and steely bouffants. There was so much smoke in the air that the ceiling seemed closer than it had that morning.

"What's your name?" I asked, realizing I hadn't read his tag earlier.

"Willard."

"Like the rat?"

"Thanks, no one's ever said that before."

"Sorry. I couldn't resist."

"The rat is named Ben, though. Willard is the guy who owns him. It's actually a good movie," he said blandly. That made me like him a little bit for some reason.

About halfway through the casino we crossed to the other side and took a short flight of stairs up to a double door with a sign over it that said, KISMET ROOM. In front of one door was a cardboard sign on an easel that had a picture of Gary Glenn and said, *Les Femmes*. Looking at Gary again I couldn't believe he wasn't a woman. Which I suppose should have made me feel better about missing something that should have been obvious.

Inside, the Kismet Room were five tiers of cabaret tables looking down at a curved stage. I followed Willard down the tiers toward a door to the right of the stage. We went through and immediately made a right and then another right. We were in a hallway with small dressing rooms on each side running parallel to the theater. Many of the doors were closed. In the open dressing rooms, there were one or two drag queens each. They gave us the hairy eyeball—extra special with false eyelashes—as we passed.

We were almost at the end when we stopped at a closed dressing room. Willard knocked, then opened the door. Gary Glenn sat at a makeup table staring at herself in a mirror, occasionally lifting a makeup brush and making a minute change to her flawless makeup. Her wig was blonde and larger than most house pets. She wore a sheer, nude gown with some strategically placed sequins. By some feat of engineering, she managed to look like a very well-endowed woman not wearing a bra. When she moved, her boobs shook and jiggled just as they should. She caught me staring.

"They're real, honey. That's why they look that way."

"Oh," was all I could think to say.

"Well, real silicone. I bought them in Beverly Hills. Twenty thousand dollars. I've got enough to do the bottom half but only if I go to Thailand. Call me racist, but I want my vagina to say 'Made in the U.S.A.'"

I wondered if that line came out of her act. Then I wondered how honest she was in her act.

"Gary, this is Nick Nowak. He's looking for Mickey Troccoli."

"I have no idea where Mickey is."

"Nick works for Jimmy English."

"In that case, I've never met Mickey Troccoli."

"Mickey's in trouble," I said. "And I'm here to get him out of it."

She looked me up and down; I don't think she liked what she saw.

"That might matter to me if I knew a Mickey Troccoli. But as I said, I don't."

"There's a problem in Chicago, the ASA made it seem like Mickey was going to be testifying against Doves. A couple of his goons are in Vegas looking for Mickey. That's the trouble I'm here to get him out of."

"I'm sorry. I don't know what you're talking about. I'm just a girl trying to make a living."

"Yeah, but you're not the only girl." I turned to Willard and asked, "Can we talk to some of the other showgirls?"

Gary's lips got thin, which was sad since she'd tried so hard to make them pouty. "Oh, what does it matter? I'm dumping him anyway," she said. "You know he wants me to leave all of this and run off to Alaska. Why would I do that?"

"So he's been staying with you?"

"Yes, yes, he's been staying with me. I'm about ready to hang him by his toes. All he can talk about is marrying me as soon as I turn a hundred percent girl. Seriously, the boy in me is getting offended."

From where I stood there wasn't a lot of boy left in her.

"Why don't you tell me where you live and I'll go see Mickey?"

"Are you crazy? I have white carpets. I'm not letting you or anyone like you near my place."

"I could look you up in the phonebook."

"You really don't think Gary Glenn is my real name, do you?"

She had me there.

"Look, Mickey is coming to pick me up after this next show. I'll get one of the other girls to take me home. He's all yours."

"Does he still drive a white Camaro with red stripes?"

"God, he loves that car."

I took that as a yes. "Where does he pick you up?"

"There's an employee entrance. I'm a little busy so you'll have to find it yourself."

"I'll show you," Willard said.

There wasn't anything else to ask her, so I said, "Don't do anything stupid like call Mickey and warn him."

"Tell Mickey I love him. And tell him I never want to see him again."

Chapter Thirteen

Willard got me a ticket and I watched Gary Glenn's *Les Femmes*. Through most of it, I thought about other things. Like, for instance, the way one thing leads to another but that doesn't necessarily make them connected. Five or six years ago, I went to a drag show with my then-boyfriend, Daniel, to see a friend of his perform. The show was horrible, compared to the one in front of me, and I got very drunk. Afterward, walking home, Daniel and I were bashed which led to my leaving the Chicago PD and our breaking up.

If that hadn't happened, I might still be on the job, I might never have become a private investigator, never have met Harker, never had met Joseph or Brian or Ross or Mrs. Harker or Terry. Yeah, I'd probably have other people in my life who mattered, but they'd be different people. And I liked the people I had.

That's the thing, though. Some bad shit happened to me and then some good shit happened to me. The good didn't happen because of the bad. No connection. Just one thing happening after another. Weird, huh?

The girls of *Les Femmes* were pretty good, I guess. They looked like real women. They looked like they were actually singing. Both things impressed the mostly straight audience. But then, Gary Glenn came on and she sang her own songs. That was actually impressive. And she could almost sing.

She did three numbers; her musical genre was innuendo. She did the Madeline Kahn song from *Blazing Saddles* about screwing too many men; *Bewitched, Bothered and Bewildered* with its original lewd lyrics; and a show tune I'd never heard about a kid who could foxtrot and every time she said foxtrot she really meant fuck. By the time she was finished it didn't matter much that Gary Glenn couldn't exactly sing.

When Gary began bringing the other girls out to take off their wigs and amaze the audience with their true sex, I slipped out the back of the theater. I went through the casino's side entrance and walked around to the back of the building, just like Willard had shown me. I passed the parking structure where I'd parked my rental, the garbage bins for the restaurants, until finally, I reached the unmarked stage door for the Kismet room. Along the edge of the property was a row of parking spaces marked for employees. The back of the casino was all jigs and jags, not meant to entice like the front entrance. I found a deep shadow and stood in it.

I lit a cigarette, figuring Mickey wasn't going to be there for at least twenty minutes. He'd know roughly when the show ended. And he'd know that it took a girl like Gary Glenn some time to change. It was good that I was early though; I wanted to be the only one waiting for Mickey.

Scanning every parked car I could see, I realized I was looking for the two guys I'd seen in court. Then it occurred to me it might not be them I was looking for. They could have easily picked up the phone and hired two other guys to take care of Mickey. So, truth be told, I didn't know who I was looking for. Two guys was all Willard had said, and I'd made the mistake of not asking what they looked like. Stupid. Very stupid.

If I knew for sure it was the guys I'd seen in the courtroom, I could assume they were driving a rental. I would also know that they knew me. If they'd sub-contracted the job I would be a stranger to whomever they hired. At some point, that might prove an advantage. Except it was one that I didn't have since I hadn't asked all the right questions. Shit.

I tried to check the time, but it was too dark in my shadow to read my Swatch. I had just finished my second cigarette, so ten or twelve minutes had passed. I checked the parked cars I could see. They were empty. A couple were models used by rental car companies. I gave those extra scrutiny. The temperature had dropped to around forty. I was wishing that I'd worn a T-shirt underneath my shirt when the white Camaro with red stripes pulled up. Even in the dim light, I could see it was bug-stained from traveling. Mickey had driven down weeks before, but I guess when you're on the lam washing your car isn't a top priority.

I left my spot in the shadows, walked directly to the passenger side of the Camaro, opened the door and dropped myself into the shotgun position. "Hungry Like the Wolf" was playing at a volume usually reserved for heavy metal. I reached over and turned it down.

"What the fuck?"

"Hello, Mickey. Long time no see."

Dressed for a date, Mickey wore a white linen jacket over a pink Izod shirt with the collar turned up, new blue jeans and a bright white pair of Reeboks. He looked roughly the same, still compact with dreamy brown eyes and straight hair. He used to have a mustache but he'd shaved it off. It made him look younger and bit surprised. Or maybe that was just the situation.

"Get out of here. I'm picking up my girlfriend."

"Yeah. He's not coming." I knew which pronouns were polite and it was time to stop being polite. "In fact, he said he never wanted to see you again."

"Shari wouldn't do that to me. She loves me."

"Yeah, his real name is Gary and when he heard you were in trouble he dumped you."

There was real hurt on his face. "You're lying."

"He didn't want you bleeding on his white carpets."

That landed. Gary must not have been lying about the white carpets.

"You need to come back to Chicago with me, Mickey."

"No, I can't do that."

"Jimmy wants you to testify. You know that don't you?"

"Yeah, I know. But I can't."

"Why not?"

"Because I can't."

"What happened, Mickey? Why did you check out of Lucky Days?"

"I moved in with my girlfriend." His voice was low and unconvincing.

"That's about the time your uncle found out you informed on Jimmy. Rumors started going around."

"A cop showed up at my door. Told me if I ever came back to Chicago I was dead."

"A cop?"

"Yeah, Devlin had friends, you know?"

I had a sudden revelation. Mickey was an important witness in Jimmy's trial. But he was also an important witness in Devlin's. ASA Sanchez knew exactly what she was doing when she said "case of this nature." She knew people would think a case like Jimmy's, and if she was ever challenged she could say she meant "high profile." Devlin's case was certainly that. There would be no ramifications for what she—

That's when the rear window of the Camaro shattered and the cassette player stopped playing because a bullet had mangled it. I pulled out my new Cheetah and fired three shots out the blown-out back window before I managed to scream, "DRIVE! FUCKING DRIVE!"

I couldn't see much of what was behind us other than a pair of headlights. Mickey floored it, throwing me against the back of my seat. I steadied myself and fired three more times. I had one bullet left and I maybe needed to keep that in reserve.

We turned onto what I thought was Sahara Avenue and were speeding east. Or maybe west. I caught a glimpse of a two-tone maroon and gray Lincoln Continental, maybe new, maybe a couple years old. And then Mickey spun the wheel and we were on a street of failing apartment buildings. It was a short block; another screeching turn and we were going east. Or at least we were going away from the casinos, so if that was east that's the way we were going.

"Keep shooting at them!"

"I only have one bullet left."

"You didn't bring more bullets?"

"I wasn't expecting you to put up a fight."

He made another turn throwing me up against the passenger door. I righted myself and then watched out the back to see if anyone made the turn with us.

"We gotta get more bullets," Mickey said.

"And we gotta get out of this car."

"No way. I love this car."

"So I've heard. It's too easy to spot."

Mickey made another turn. We were still in a sort of residential area, but it didn't seem like anyone was following us.

"If we can get back to Lucky Days I have ammo there and a rental car."

"I'll drop you off," he said.

"No. We're sticking together. Look, you can leave your car in the garage there and get it another time." *Like never,* I thought. "They're not going to think we're stupid enough to go back to the hotel. Not right away."

Mickey made a sharp turn and cut back out to Sahara. Quickly we were turning right onto Las Vegas Blvd. This part I was familiar with. I was even pretty sure we were going north.

As we got near the hotel, I said, "Pull into the front and give your car to the valet."

"Are you kidding? They charge five bucks. And you gotta tip 'em."

"It's on me."

"What if I don't want to go with you? What if I want to drop you off?"

"I've got a gun, Mickey. And I've still got one bullet."

"You're not gonna kill me. You're not that sort."

"Do you have a gun?"

And then he got it. He was safer with me than without me, at least for the moment. He pulled the car under Lucky Days' sprawling awning. I waited for him to get out of the car first. I'm not the trusting sort. As soon as I saw him toss his keys to the scrawny kid in the green-and-gold jacket, I jumped out.

"Hey! What happened to your window?" the valet yelled after us.

But we were already bolting into the casino. Once through the door, I slowed us down. Trying not to be too obvious, I scanned the place as we walked through. Nothing. It took forever for an elevator to come all the way down. When it did, Mickey and I hopped in and so did another eight people. They were all young, kids practically, with drinks in their hands. It was annoying that they were slowing us down. I wanted to get out of there. But I was also pretty sure the kids didn't work for Doves. Or the Chicago PD for that matter.

We got to sixteen and hurried down the hallway to my room, I opened the door and we walked in. Since I'd packed everything up earlier, I went right to my suitcase on the bed and opened it up. I'd put the extra ammo into the elastic flap sewn into the top of the case. I popped the magazine out of the Cheetah and filled it with bullets.

"Hey, why don't we just stay here for a while," Mickey said.

"It's not safe here."

"Who knows you're here?"

"The front desk."

"But…nobody knows who you are."

"Yeah, they do. I've been sitting with the defense at Jimmy's trial. I'm sure people know who I am."

"I gotta think, okay. I need some time."

"It's a four-hour flight to Chicago. You'll have plenty of time to think." Which made me wonder when the next flight out to Chicago might be. I finished loading my gun. Put it back in my holster and closed up my suitcase. I sat down on the bed and picked up the phone. I got an outside line and dialed information. When the operator came on I asked for Frontier Airlines and she connected me.

"I want to see Shari before I leave."

"He won't like that."

"Don't be that way. You don't know what we got."

"What did you think was going to happen, Mickey? Did you think the two of you would just run off into the sun—" Someone picked up at Frontier. "Yeah, hello, I need to get a flight out of McCarren to O'Hare tonight." Then I realized it was well after midnight. "This morning I mean."

I was told that the last flight out had happened twenty minutes before and that there weren't any flights out until six ten the next morning. After I said, 'are you sure' a few times, I asked if there were seats available on the six ten and was told the plane was half empty. I decided not to make a reservation because something was falling into place, something important.

If I got Mickey back to Chicago on Saturday what was I going to do with him? I couldn't bring him home to Joseph and Ross, not while there were people out to kill him. Maybe it was better to get on that last flight out on Sunday night and bring him right to court. I wasn't sure if that was a good plan or even what might be a good plan, but I did know one thing. "We have to get out of here."

I grabbed the suitcase and led Mickey out of the room. If I'd given more thought to what I was going to do with Mickey once I found him I'd have brought a pair of handcuffs. As it was, I didn't have too much more than logic to coax him along and I wasn't sure he was the kind of guy logic worked on. In the elevator, I hit the button for the second floor. As the elevator started, Mickey reached over and pressed the button marked CASINO.

"You hit the wrong button," he said.

"If they're in the building they might be waiting by the elevator. We're getting off at two and taking the stairs." There was only a small chance they'd be waiting, but it wasn't a chance I wanted to take. Besides, fear might be the best way to control Mickey. I might be wise to keep him terrorized. Hell, I was scared shitless so it wouldn't be hard.

When we got to the second floor, we dashed out of the elevator and then followed exit signs to the stairs. The stairwell was another world. Where the hotel was thoughtfully decorated with colorful carpet and rich wallpaper, the stairwell was all concrete and metal painted the color of a sand trap. We banged down the stairs to the first floor, but instead of finding a door that opened into the casino we were in a long hallway going God knows where. We hurried along and about a hundred feet down found a door leading outside. I didn't know what was on the other side of the door, but I figured it wouldn't be someone trying to kill us. If I didn't know where we were then neither did they.

Outside, we found ourselves in the same employee parking area that we'd started in. The parking garage was to the right, with an entrance at the corner. We'd only take a few steps toward it when I saw the lights. Blue and red flashing lights that seemed to be coming from the entrance of the parking garage. Mickey stopped in his tracks.

"Something happened. We have to come up with another plan."

"No, I think this is fine. The lights are the Las Vegas police. They don't have a reason to bother us, do they?"

He shook his head.

"They look kind of busy."

I didn't want to think too hard about what might be keeping them busy. I managed to get Mickey moving again and a few minutes later, we were in the Pontiac and I was pulling out of the space. Both of us were on edge. We really had no idea what we were about to encounter. I drove down to the second floor and just as we were about to descend to the first floor we were in a traffic jam. There were four cars stopped in front of us.

We could just barely see the entrance to the parking garage. A half dozen police officers were standing around Mickey's Camaro. Their squads sat right outside the parking structure, lights flashing turning the white Camaro pink, then baby blue, then pink again. It looked like the car had been driven into the wall. The passenger door was open. The cars in front of us blocked most of my view, but I could see a hand on the ground and the sleeve of a green-and-gold jacket.

Chapter Fourteen

The Sunbeam Motel had about fifty rooms on two floors. There was no magician, no revue, no buffet. The only features they had to boast about on their sign were a huge swimming pool, air-conditioning and PAY TV. It was two lots down from the Marina Hotel, I'd driven by it on the way to Lucky Days. When we checked in, I gave the night clerk two hundred and twenty-five dollars for Friday, Saturday and Sunday nights. I was only planning to stay part of that, but I didn't want to be kicked out before it was convenient. When the clerk asked for a credit card to cover incidentals, I added seventy-five dollars and told him anything left over was his for the taking. His eyes lit up like little neon signs. Not surprising given our location. I signed the guest register for both of us: Donald and Martin Osmond from Spokane.

I'd say the best thing about the room itself was that it was clean, except that if you looked closely it wasn't. So, the best thing about the room was that nobody knew we were there and it was going to be challenging for anyone to find us. Not getting shot at is an under-appreciated luxury.

There were two queen-sized beds, both with a polyester bedspread in autumn colors, a large portable TV sitting on a chipped mahogany dresser, and a wooden café table with two chairs. I dumped my suitcase into one the chairs and flopped onto a bed. Mickey stood by the door and said, "I'm hungry."

"You'll be able to eat in a couple hours. Continental breakfast comes with the room."

"Shari and I go to dinner after her show. There's a Chinese place in the MGM Grand that's open all night."

"That's nice. I think we'll stay here." I kicked off my penny loafers. "Sit down. Make yourself comfortable."

"I don't want to stay here."

"You're safe here, Mickey. You're not safe anywhere else."

"It's a big city. How would they know if we went to the MGM? How would they know we were at the Chinese place?"

"They probably wouldn't know."

"So why can't we go?"

"Because there's a chance they might. And if they do, you're dead. Just like the valet."

I could tell he wanted to keep arguing, just like I could tell he wanted to go to the Chinese place at the MGM hoping to find Gary Glenn, but he didn't want to end up like the poor kid who'd tried to park his car. When we finally were able to drive out of the parking garage, we got a good look at the Camaro riddled with bullet holes and the kid on the floor of the garage partly covered by a sheet.

I sat up and started taking my clothes off.

"What are you doing?"

"I'm getting ready for bed. It's late."

"I'm not going to have sex with you. I'm in love with Shari."

"Did I make a pass at you?"

I was down to my boxers so I stopped stripping. Mickey hadn't moved. Obviously, he wasn't tired and, in fact, was pretty freaked out. And why wouldn't he be? Of course, he wasn't going to sleep anytime soon and that meant neither was I.

"Let's talk about how all this happened."

"All what happened?"

"This. You. You with your car all shot up hiding from Doves' guys."

"I don't know how it happened."

"The owner of Dresden put it in a complaint that got you picked up by Devlin."

"I didn't know the part about the guy from Dresden. Those cops, they beat the shit out of a guy and they ask a lot of questions. They don't do a lot of explaining."

"They made you inform on Jimmy."

"I guess."

"You guess? You mean you're not sure?"

"Yeah. They did that. They wrote it all down. Called it an interview. Made me sign it. Shit, I didn't even read it."

"Why did they let you go? Why didn't they keep you hidden?"

"They didn't want Jimmy to know. They said I should go back to doing what I did and keep my mouth shut. But I'm not stupid. They think I'm stupid but I'm not. I went and told Jimmy."

"What did Jimmy say?"

"He needed to think about it. Then a few days later the Camaro showed up in my parents' driveway. There was a note from Jimmy that said to keep doing what I was doing and to tell everybody he gave me the car."

That was kind of funny. About the Camaro. Jimmy had once given me a car. It was used but it also had stripes. I was sensing a theme.

"So that's what you did until I came by and told you to get out of town."

"Yeah. Jimmy thought I should go. That people would know you found out I talked to Devlin about him."

"And then what?"

"I came to Vegas and fell in love."

"You can tell me that story later. Why did you leave Lucky Days?"

"Everyone found out I'd ratted Jimmy out. Oh man, I should have let them beat me to death, you know? I mean, I'm just gonna end up dead anyway. What's the point of dragging it out?"

I didn't want him talking like that. It was going to be hard enough keeping him alive without a bad attitude. "For one thing you got to fall in love. For another you're not dead yet. Do you know how everyone found out you informed on Jimmy?"

"Something about his trial. Everyone thinks I'm gonna testify against Jimmy. Everyone's afraid of what I'm gonna say. And then that cop showed up at the hotel. It didn't seem smart to be so easy to find."

He'd still been pretty easy to find.

"Okay. Here's the thing, Mickey. Devlin's friends want to get you. And Doves wants to get you. The only way you can save yourself is to stand up in court and tell the truth about Devlin. Then there won't be any point in Devlin's friends being after you; you'll have done your worst, and Doves will know you're not out to get him. The only way to save yourself is to testify."

There might have been a few holes in my logic, but I decided not to see them and hope that Mickey didn't see them either. Mickey sat down on the other bed.

"Jimmy will make sure you're okay," I said, though I wasn't too sure of that either.

"Jimmy's not going to live forever. What happens then?"

"By then it's long over. Once Devlin goes to jail and once Doves knows you're not going to inform on him, you'll be fine."

Mickey was buying it. I was almost buying it myself. I mean, he was a small piece in a big game. It didn't make much sense to kill him. If you're gonna kill, kill the big pieces.

"I don't got no pajamas," he said.

I guess that meant he was finally getting tired.

I didn't sleep much. Just before sunrise, Mickey crawled into bed with me. I grumbled, "Hey...thought you didn't wanna have sex with me."

"I don't. I'm lonely. I miss my fiancée."

I could have tried explaining that I wasn't all that much like his fiancée but on the other hand parts of me were. He rolled over onto his face, threw an arm over my chest and fell back to sleep. I lay there trapped beneath him for about an hour with my mind racing. I was *pretty* sure we were safe. I tested that theory over and over again. I was *pretty* sure if I were looking for us I wouldn't be able to find us. Neither name was on the motel registration. No one knew what I was driving. We were two guys in their late twenties to mid-thirties staying in a hotel room together. My guess was that was happening all over Vegas for a whole raft of reasons. So, I was *pretty* sure we were fine.

But I wasn't absolutely sure.

Around eight, I slipped out from under Mickey to go down to the office to get us some of the continental breakfast we'd been promised. It was chilly out; I don't think it was even sixty degrees. The sky was a bright polished blue and somehow seemed bigger than it did in Chicago. There was a nice crispness in the air that made it seem possible that a Midwestern boy like me could live in the desert. Of course, the minute it hit a hundred and ten I'd be packing up and heading home.

In the office, a tablecloth had been spread over a card table and a selection of day-old Danish, straggly bacon, hard-boiled eggs, orange juice and bagels were artlessly spread out. A toaster sat in one corner of the table. I cooked up two bagels; spread them with cream cheese, then piled them onto a plate with a couple Danish, four eggs and half the bacon they'd put out. I turned around and saw that the day clerk, a middle-aged woman in a heavy avocado-colored sweater she'd probably made herself, was staring a hole through me.

"It's not just for me," I said.

"It's a continental breakfast. Not a buffet."

"Oh, I know. You should see me at a buffet."

I poured two Styrofoam cups three-quarters full of coffee and juggled it all back to the room. Unable to open the door I kicked it a couple time. A moment later, Mickey opened the door. He was groggy, hair askew, tighty whities grabbing at his morning boner. In other words, totally fuckable. I pushed by him and brought breakfast over to the café table. He closed the door.

"Lock it," I told him.

He did.

"And when I'm not here, don't answer it."

"But I knew it was you."

"How?"

"You were gone."

"Exactly why you shouldn't open the door."

"Shut up. Okay? Nobody died."

He scratched his crotch then got embarrassed about his hard on. He walked over to the table and sat down. I put my open suitcase onto the floor and sat down to eat. "I'll loan you a clean T-shirt."

"Why? Are we going somewhere?"

"You want to sit around for two days in dirty clothes that's up to you."

"So we're staying here until Monday?"

"We're going to take a red-eye Sunday night. That will put us in Chicago right before court."

He didn't say anything. I was afraid he might backslide and insist on staying in Las Vegas. But he didn't. He came over to the table and sullenly began to eat his breakfast. I got up and turned the TV on, flipping the channels until I got the local news. Then I sat back down and ate a stale bagel.

"Do we have to watch that?"

"Just for a few minutes. Then we can watch a movie on Home Box Office."

"I've seen it."

"You don't even know what it is."

"I own a video store, remember?"

I was pretty sure he ran a video store for his uncle, which was different than owning one, but this wasn't the day to argue with him.

"Well, we'll try to find something you haven't seen."

"Not gonna happen. Video comes before pay TV. I've seen everything."

"Then we'll watch something you've seen. You can tell me everything that's going to happen and ruin it for me."

He scowled at me. Just then the TV got my attention. "A valet at Lucky Days casino was gunned down this morning at around 1:30 a.m. Donald Goudy of Henderson, nineteen, was parking a car belonging to a hotel guest when a passing vehicle opened fire. The young man was taken to the hospital but could not be revived. Police are searching for the owner of the white Camaro Goudy was attempting to park when he was shot."

They showed an angle on the parking garage at Lucky Days from across the street.

"Holy shit," Mickey said.

That was all I wanted to see, so I flipped the dial until I found Home Box Office. It was playing a movie with two of the guys from *Saturday Night Live.*

"It's our fault that kid died," Mickey said.

I wasn't sure what to say to that. Choices we made certainly led to the kid getting killed, but we didn't know that when we made them. We didn't know the guys who were after Mickey would shoot the car up without checking to see who they were shooting at. It wasn't our fault, but it sure felt like it was. So I had a lot of trouble disagreeing.

We ate in silence. It was depressing to think about that poor dead kid. It was depressing to think it could have been us. Or at least Mickey. I watched him eat a bagel. There was cream cheese on his face. I motioned that he should wipe his face.

"You wanna fuck?" he asked, wiping cream cheese off his face.

"What about your girlfriend?"

"You're an asshole, you know that?"

"I have some idea, yes."

"So you wanna fuck or not?"

"Sure. Let's fuck."

We didn't move right away. Mickey ate the rest of his bagel, then used the bottom of this T-shirt to wipe his mouth. He got up and walked back over to the bed. As he did, he dropped his briefs and pulled his T-shirt over this head. His butt was as pert as I remembered and jiggled nicely as he crossed the room.

He lay on the bed face down, then pushed a pillow beneath him so that his ass popped up into the air. I knew what he was doing. He was using me, using sex so that he didn't have to think about anything. I suppose if I were looking for love in the eyes of every guy I fucked, I'd have been offended. But I wasn't.

I dug through my suitcase until I found the condoms Joseph had put there. I took them and the lube and set them on the nightstand between the beds. When Mickey saw them he said, "You don't need those. It ruins it."

"Guilt and fear ruin it, too."

He thought about it for the briefest second and said, "Jesus Christ. Whatever."

I stepped out of my clothes and got onto the bed with him. I ran a finger down the crack of his ass, letting it linger around his hole. I kissed each of his ass cheeks. Then ran my tongue down the path my finger had traveled. Mickey shivered and said, "Oh my God."

I teased him with my tongue until he was pushing his hips into my face, then I slipped a finger into his spit-lubed ass. I pressed down where I thought his prostate would be. A moan told me I'd found it. I rubbed the spot a while and then slipped a second finger into him. Moving them in and out, I slowly widened them. And then I slipped in a third. I didn't get too far with that before he was demanding, "Come on, guy, fuck me."

Grabbing the tube of KY, I rubbed a tiny bit on my dick and then a lot more on his butt. I opened up one of the condoms and then rolled it onto my hard dick. I spread Mickey's cheeks and pushed into him. Even with the condom, it felt okay. Without a condom, it would have been sending shivers through me, but with the condom, I could still feel how tightly his ass clenched me. I moved in and out slowly a few times and then after he wiggled his ass in frustration, I began to pound him as hard as I could.

I had hold of him by his hips, slamming him. He was moaning and groaning, but then dropped that for a kind of low keening. I tried to reach under him to jack him off but he pushed my hand away. That annoyed me. I was the one in charge, but he seemed to think he was.

Slowing down, I pulled my dick very nearly all the way out. To tease him, I pushed the head of my dick back in and then slowly pulled it almost all the way out. I had the feeling it was one of those moves that guys hated and loved at the same time. Mickey was starting to bitch, but he didn't do anything to stop me from being inside of him.

I decided then to give him exactly what he wanted: your basic piston move. I could tell that's what he wanted because the minute I started he began saying, "Yeah, yeah, that's it, yeah." I kept it up, as hard and as fast as I could manage, hoping one of us would come soon. Well, kind of hoping it would be me. Squeezing my eyes shut, I focused on what I was doing, the feel of Mickey's ass cheeks in my hands, the simple uncomplicated act of fucking him and then I felt him start, his sphincter suddenly grabbing onto me, squeezing tight and that did it. I was coming, squirting into the condom. Twice. Three times.

I'd just pulled out of him and rolled off, and was thinking I should ask whether he came when he said, "I miss my Shari."

I resisted the urge to correct him and say, "Gary."

Chapter Fifteen

We ordered pizza delivered for lunch and then had a long argument about whether or not we could lay in the sun by the pool—he was for, I was against. After he gave up, Mickey discovered a sitcom on HBO I'd never heard of, *Brothers*. It was about these three brothers. One of them was gay, so it was mainly about how the other two reacted. It was kind of like listening to Archie Bunker and Maude getting together and talking about gay shit. I made it through one episode.

While he watched TV, I paged Owen and waited for him to call. *Brothers* had ended by then and Mickey was watching *Footloose* for the fifth time.

"Why would anyone want Bacon as a last name?" he asked. "It's like being named Sausage or Ham."

The phone rang and I was saved from answering him.

"I'm here with Mickey," I told Owen. "We're going to be coming back tomorrow night on the red-eye."

"Darling you're a gem. What time are you getting in?"

"I'm not sure. I haven't booked the flight. There's one at twelve forty-five. That would get us to the courthouse around seven Chicago time."

"That's perfect. Court starts at ten, that'll give us time with Mickey. I'll get there early and find us a room."

"This hasn't been easy."

"I can't imagine it has been."

"We got shot at. Couple of Doves' guys I think."

"That's distressing."

"We ditched Mickey's car with a valet and they killed the kid thinking he was Mickey. Nineteen."

"That's terrible."

"Now the police are looking for Mickey."

"So they'll be keeping an eye on the airport."

"Yeah, maybe."

"What airline are you taking?"

"Probably Frontier."

"I'll make a couple of reservations for Mickey on other airlines earlier in the day. If they're watching the airport they'll be plenty bored by the time you do show up."

I was sure we'd be just fine. We'd head to the airport at the last possible minute, buy our tickets, and go right to the gate and board. If there wasn't much more than fifteen minutes between the time we bought our tickets and the time the plane took off, there wouldn't be enough time to nab to us.

Besides, it was hard to say how much they really wanted Mickey. Yeah, they had his car, but they might know he couldn't tell them much. I was pretty sure the casino had lots of security cameras. They were very likely piecing together Mickey and my movements through the casino. That would tell them we didn't see anything. Sure, they still needed to talk to Mickey, just not enough to stake out the airport.

"We need to make sure Mickey is safe when all this is over."

"Of course."

I would have liked it better if instead of simply agreeing he'd mentioned how we were going to do it. On the other hand, I didn't want to have a long discussion about it in front of Mickey. I hung up and then got on the bed with Mickey.

We had sex two more times. Each time was pretty much the same. He liked to be face down, ass in the air. He didn't like to kiss. He didn't like to suck cock. Both of which would have made it a much more pleasant experience for me. After the second time, I asked him, "How come you don't want to look at me while we're fucking?"

"Why would I want to look at a guy fucking me?"

"Mickey, I think you like guys."

"Guys are okay if there are no girls around."

"Shari's not a girl."

"She will be. When we go to Thailand." I had serious doubts about how Mickey might feel about Shari once she was a hundred percent woman from top to bottom.

"And then what?"

"Then we live happily ever after like normal people. Get a house. Have some kids. You know, normal shit."

I was kind of stunned. I mean, he seemed to think he and Gary Glenn were going to have some kind of *Make Room for Daddy* life someday. Gary Glenn might someday be Shari Glenn, but she wouldn't be having kids and wouldn't be adopting them either. I wasn't even sure the marriage would be legal. And I certainly knew she wouldn't stop being a female impersonator. Even if the impersonation did become more truth than impression.

"So do you have AIDS? Is that why you gotta use a condom?" he asked me out of the blue.

"I'm not sick," I said. It was the truth, but it didn't

really answer his question.

"But you think you've got it, right?" Mickey said.

"I guess so."

I could almost hear him deciding whether or not to worry about that. He was tense for a few moments. Then he seemed to relax completely, probably when he realized he was likely to die long before he could catch anything from me.

"What do you think happens after a person dies?" he asked.

"I don't know. I guess I'll find out when it happens to me."

"You gotta have some idea."

"Maybe nothing happens. Or maybe something wonderful. I don't know."

"It might be something bad. I mean, there's a hell, right?"

"If there's a hell, we're already there."

"Jesus, that's cheerful."

"What? You want me to tell you that if you end up dead, it doesn't matter because you'll be in heaven floating on a cloud?"

"I don't think I'll go to heaven. I'm not such a great guy."

"You're not so bad. There are a lot worse people." That was faint praise.

My opinion of Mickey was changing. When I first met him six months before, I thought he was not that sharp and a maybe a little dangerous. I still didn't think he was all that sharp. On the one hand, I think he'd been smart to go to Jimmy after Devlin beat information out of him. But then thinking Gary Glenn was going to have babies and keep house for him was just plain dumb. Dangerous, though, Mickey wasn't. One time he said that if people didn't pay up he'd threaten them and then tell Jimmy. Mickey wasn't what you'd call muscle. He had muscles—nice muscles—he just wasn't the sort to use them. They were decorative, not dangerous.

I wanted to call home and talk to Joseph. I didn't, though, because Mickey was making noise again about calling Gary Glenn. I didn't want him to, and that made calling my boyfriend in front of him hard to justify. I didn't think Joseph would worry too much. The death of a parking attendant wouldn't make national news, so the only thing that might make him worry was my not calling. He'd probably figure that I hadn't found Mickey yet and was trying hard to do that.

Mickey and I spent forty-five minutes debating about what kind of take-out to order. I found a Chinese place and we ordered Kung Pao chicken and shrimp fried rice. Since I was working my way through the yellow pages, I called around until I found a store that delivered, Knee-High Beverage. I ordered a bottle of Johnnie Walker, two six packs of Miller, a carton of Marlboro reds, a couple bags of potato chips, onion dip and, at Mickey's request, two packages of Oreos. An hour later we were stuffing ourselves. I'd forgotten to ask for plastic forks, so Mickey and I struggled to eat our dinners with chopsticks passing the paper containers back and forth.

Afterward, we read our fortunes. Mine said, "Remember that tomorrow, today will be yesterday." I had no idea what that could mean. I'd actually been hoping for a fortune with a little luck in it. Mickey's said, "Beware of woman with heart of sand." His made sense to me. I could see from the look on his face he was trying not to come to that same conclusion.

Full of scotch, Oreos and Chinese food, I drifted off while we were watching *Splash*. The movie must have reminded Mickey of his own mismatched romance, because I woke up after the movie to the sound of him crying into the phone.

"But I didn't do anything wrong, Shari. I don't know how I'm going to live without you."

I pretended I was still asleep.

###

Sunday morning I was nervous and jumpy. There was a digital clock on the nightstand reading 8:46 a.m. That meant it was almost eleven in Chicago. In less than twenty-four hours, this whole thing would be over. All I had to do was get Mickey safely out of Las Vegas and then from O'Hare to the courthouse in one piece. I might have been calmer if we could have gotten the show on the road, but I had another fourteen, fifteen hours before we could even start. That was a lot of time to stare at a guy I barely knew who only liked to be fucked face down.

I walked to the office and picked up our continental breakfast. It was pretty much the same fare as the day before, except there were bran muffins instead of Danishes. At least I thought they were bran muffins. They might have been some kind of rock gathered out in the desert. The same middle-aged woman stared a hole in my back. I turned around and smiled. Today she was wearing an aquamarine cardigan featuring a stitch she hadn't quite mastered.

"The girlfriend has a big appetite."

"You don't have a girl in there."

That wasn't good. I didn't like that she was paying attention. And I sure didn't like the nasty look on her face. I put our breakfast down and reached into my pocket for a twenty. I held it out to her saying, "Privacy is a very valuable thing."

She ignored my money. "Ain't your brother neither."

"Our parents will be disappointed to hear that."

"And you definitely ain't no Osmonds."

"It's a big family. We breed like rabbits."

"This is my place. My nephew let you in here. You come in the daytime we would have been full up. You get my meaning?"

"Yeah, I think your meaning is pretty clear."

Mrs. Sunbeam hated fags. In a way, that was a relief. For a moment I'd been afraid one of Doves' guys had called looking for two guys on the run. If they had she would have told them all about us. So they hadn't called. Yet. If they didn't call during her shift, then we'd be home free. I was tempted to ask when she got off.

"Don't get any ideas about extending your stay," she said.

"We won't. Don't worry."

I put the twenty back into my jeans, poured two cups of coffee, balanced them in one hand, picked up our continental breakfast, and backed out of the lobby. I walked back to the room as carefully as possible, only spilling a tiny bit of scalding coffee onto my wrist.

Setting everything on the café table, I went to the spare bed and picked up my gun and holster. I checked the gun to make sure I'd filled the cartridge. I had, I knew I had, but I had to check anyway. After I holstered the gun, I sat down and lit a cigarette. My gut said we shouldn't stay there. Not with that woman down there sitting next to a telephone all day.

I ate a hard-boiled egg and a bit of bacon. Took a bite of the bran muffin, but decided not to risk breaking a tooth. After I ate there was nothing to do but watch Mickey sleep. Patience was not a strong point of mine. Staying at the motel all day was either the best decision I could make or the worst. And I had to figure out which it was. That wasn't going to happen sitting there listening to Mickey's soft snoring. I put on my jacket and went back down to the office.

Breakfast ended at nine and had already been packed up. The card table was now covered with glossy brochures. Mrs. Sunbeam had a tiny black-and-white TV set up on the counter. She was watching Jimmy Swaggart. When I walked through the door she gave me a dirty look. I ignored it and studied the brochures on the card table.

They were for places like Bonnie Springs Ranch, Hoover Dam, Lake Mead, some golf course, a place you could ride a horse, an auto collection at one of the casinos.

"So if I wanted to do something today that wasn't gambling, what would you suggest?"

"Go back where you came from."

"Without leaving town." I smiled at her. I hoped it was a friendly smile, but that might have been asking too much. "How far is it to the Hoover Dam?"

"Forty-five minutes. An hour if you can't read a map."

"Sounds like fun."

"Why?"

"I like water." We glared at each other for a moment, then I asked, "Has anyone called about us?" It was a risky thing to ask but not being sure whether she'd gotten a phone call was a scab I just had to pick. When her eyes flashed the tiniest bit and her mouth tightened, I knew.

"Why would anyone call about you?"

"We got these friends, they like to play practical jokes. That's why we don't tell them where we are. They show up, get drunk and piss in the pool. That kind of thing. They might call around trying to find us."

"The pool is for guests only. Make sure your friends know that."

I could barely breathe for a moment. I was pretty sure that meant she'd gotten the phone call I was worried about.

"You know what, if our friends do show up tell them we went to the Hoover Dam and we won't be back until late."

"I ain't your secretary."

"No, you're not."

I hurried back down to the room. As soon as I got through the door, I shook Mickey's feet and said, "You need to pack."

He squinted at me and said, "But I don't got nothing."

That had slipped my mind.

"Take a shower then, we're leaving."

Mickey didn't need to be told twice. He hurried out of bed and went into the bathroom. I changed into a blue and yellow plaid Colours shirt Joseph had gotten me at Fields. I wiggled back into the holster and then put my old corduroy jacket on over it. Quickly, I threw the rest of my things into my suitcase. It didn't take long. I hadn't taken much out of it. I went into the bathroom to get my toothbrush and a couple other things. Mickey was already out of the shower drying off.

"What's going on?"

"I think Doves' guys know where we are."

He nodded and threw the towel aside. I followed him back out to the room and watched while he put on his jeans and a T-shirt I'd loaned him. He didn't bother with underwear. He'd been wearing the one pair for two days already.

"Come on, let's go," he said, grabbing his sneakers.

Outside, the car was parked in front of the room. I lifted up the hatch and threw my suitcase in behind the seat. Then I walked around and got in. Mickey was tying his sneakers as I pulled onto Las Vegas Boulevard going north. Of course, I had no intention of going to Hoover Dam. I was crossing my fingers that Mrs. Sunbeam would tell Doves' guys we'd gone there, and they'd either go there to find us or wait at the motel for us to come back.

"Where are we going?" Mickey asked.

"I don't know."

"Can we—"

"No. You need to leave Shari alone. Call her in a couple days after things have calmed down."

"Then why don't we just go to the airport?"

"Because right now we got two guys looking for us. In Chicago, there could be dozens."

"So are we going to check into another hotel?"

"Duck!" I hissed at him. We were at the intersection of Las Vegas Boulevard and Flamingo Road, in the center lane two cars back. Across the intersection on Las Vegas Boulevard coming toward us, I could see a maroon and gray Lincoln Continental. At twenty-one, twenty-two grand each, there couldn't be a lot of those floating around. Mickey was scrunched onto the floor. I put on my blinker and stuck the nose of the car into the middle lane. Somehow I had to get over to the far lane so we could turn. I looked in the rearview mirror; it was still early so there wasn't a whole lot of traffic. Just enough to make this difficult.

The light turned green and I jumped lanes cutting off a beat-up Chevelle from the sixties. Gritting my teeth I veered into the first lane, causing a Coupe DeVille to screech to a halt and punch his horn. I got turned onto Flamingo Road. I had no idea if the Lincoln had seen us. The fact that we got honked at didn't make me happy, though.

We weren't on Flamingo Road long. I made a snap decision and cut into a small alley that had a big sign for the Flamingo Casino—featuring a $3.45 buffet—on one side, and a small casino/liquor store called Stage Door on the other. I drove by the parking garage for the Flamingo to the one for the pagoda-themed Imperial Plaza.

I was pretty sure the car collection was at this casino and it seemed as good a place as any for us to cool our heels for a while. Inside the parking garage, I told Mickey he could sit up again. I hadn't seen anything that suggested the Lincoln had followed us or that they'd even seen us. Still, I wasn't taking any chances.

When we parked on the third floor, I walked around to the back of the wannabe Chevette, opened the hatch and took out my suitcase. I tossed in the keys to both the car and our hotel room, then I shut the hatch.

"You think they saw the car?" Mickey asked.

"I don't know. If they didn't then the woman at The Sunbeam Motel will tell them what we're driving."

"How would she know?"

"It's been sitting in front of our room for two days. And she's nosey."

"What are we going to do here?"

"I don't know. Go look at some cars. Have some lunch. Wander around."

"Yesterday you thought that was a bad idea."

"That was yesterday. Now I think sitting in a hotel room is a bad idea."

"You have no idea what you're doing. You're gonna get me killed."

"Look, maybe they saw us. Maybe they knew it was us. Hey, maybe they even saw us turn into the alley for the Flamingo. But they don't know we drove by it. So they're gonna drive all over the place looking for this car. Or maybe they didn't see us and they're down at the motel being told we went to Hoover Dam. So we're gonna go look at this car museum for an hour or so. By that time they'll have looked around and gone away."

"Why won't they come to the car museum?"

"Put yourself in their shoes. You just found the car; where do you look next?"

He thought about it. Thought hard. He wanted to say up to see the cars but he couldn't. "I guess I'd think you walked through the casino and got a cab."

"Exactly. Come on."

It took a little maneuvering but we found our way to the Auto Collection, which was on the top floor of the parking garage. It cost two dollars each to look at a hundred cars. A lot of the cars were boring as shit, but Mickey was impressed by an 1886 Mercedes, "No way, this is a car? It looks like a buggy."

"That's why they called them horseless carriages."

"Oh."

Next to it was a 1963 Lincoln Continental convertible used by JFK. "This isn't—"

"No, it's a different one."

My personal favorite was a red-and-white Ford Ranchero from the late fifties. It was just plain classy. When we were done staring at the cars we'd killed forty-five minutes and stretched out my right arm carrying the blue suitcase from car to car. My Swatch said it was one-fifteen in Chicago so that made it eleven-fifteen. Almost time for lunch. But then Mickey reminded me he hadn't had breakfast, so it was time for brunch.

We took the elevators down to the casino and wandered around until we found a set of escalators leading up to the weirdly named Teahouse Coffee Shop. The buffet might have been cheaper, but Mickey wanted breakfast and I was ready for lunch. The Teahouse was quiet. It had that going for it. The décor was Chinese, Japanese or general Asian; I honestly couldn't tell which. We were shown to a black lacquered booth and given menus. There was nothing remotely Asian about the menu. Mickey ordered steak and eggs, I had a grilled ham and cheese with French fries. After lunch, we walked down to the Flamingo, practically next door. We played dollar blackjack for about an hour. I won enough to cover breakfast, but Mickey lost the twenty I gave him to play with.

Then we wandered around the hotel until we found a men's store called Rudolpho's. Most of the clothes in there were terrible; too bright, too silky, too casual. But I had to get something for Mickey to wear to court. He was wearing a black T-shirt with Michael Jackson moonwalking on the chest. Brian had bought it for me as a joke when he and Franklin went and saw the Jacksons' Victory tour at Comiskey Park. I didn't really get the joke, but it was comfortable to sleep in. I didn't think Judge Corbin would get the joke either, so we needed something else.

It took a while, but we found a black linen jacket, a white rayon shirt and a red tie. He'd have to go with jeans and sneakers. This was the best we could do. We walked around the Flamingo for a while, Mickey carrying the bag from Rudolpho's and me carrying the blue suitcase. Anywhere else and we would have stuck out like sore thumbs. In Vegas though, no one cared.

When I noticed a bank of three phone booths by the restrooms we stopped there. The phones weren't too far from the cashier's cage. Presumably, so you could call someone to bring you more cash when you ran out. I made Mickey stand where I could see him and called a couple airlines. TWA, Frontier and United all had flights leaving after midnight: 12:10, 12:36 and 12:42. All had available seats. All we needed to do was take a cab to the airport, plunk down my credit card and then run to catch a flight.

We had ten hours to kill.

Chapter Sixteen

We got into a cab around eleven-thirty. Mickey and I were both exhausted from floating around all day. We gambled some more, first cards and then slots. Mickey was still carrying a plastic bucket filled with quarters when we got into the cab. After we gambled we ate again. Steaks. Mickey had a couple beers, I decided we were safer if I stayed sober.

Mickey was quiet most of the day. I wasn't sure which was bugging him more, the break-up with Gary Glenn or the possibility of being killed before we got to court the next day. Either way, he seemed to have given up. He stopped mentioning Shari née Gary and did whatever I told him to. In the long run, his surrender was probably not good. In the short run, I appreciated it.

After dinner, we gambled some more and then crossed the street to walk around Caesars for a while. We found a souvenir shop and bought black baseball hats that said Caesars Palace on the front in gold thread. I also picked up an ashtray and a couple packs of cards to give to Brian and Ross. For Joseph, I got a coffee mug.

In the cab, I opened my suitcase and put the bag of souvenirs inside, then I put the Cheetah in and closed it.

That made me nervous. I wasn't happy about floating around Las Vegas all day, but I'd had my gun the whole time. The airport was the most likely place we might run into Doves' guys again. I could only hope that they believed my ruse and were sitting outside the Sunbeam Motel waiting for us to come back from Hoover Dam.

The cab pulled up in front of the terminal. I paid the driver and Mickey and I scrambled out. It was five minutes until midnight. Inside, the terminal was empty except for a handful of reservation agents and a Moonie in a yellow robe wandering around aimlessly. That was good. I liked empty.

We tried the American Airlines desk first.

"You have a flight to Chicago leaving at 12:10? Are there two seats?"

The agent was a young girl, pretty, uncomfortable in the polyester maroon uniform with its coordinating scarf. She clicked some keys on the CRT. Not nearly enough it seemed. She looked up and said, "Yes, there are seats available. You can just make it. Name please?"

"Nowak, Nick. This is Michelangelo Troccoli."

"Just Mickey, okay."

She began typing in my name or Mickey's, I wasn't sure when suddenly she stopped. "Oh, hold on…"

I didn't like that. Doves' guys couldn't stop us at the airport but ASA Sanchez might be able to. But then the girl said, "You're already on this flight. Did you make a reservation earlier today?"

"It was made for us. I just wasn't sure."

"Okay, well, this speeds things up." She hit a few more buttons and our tickets and boarding passes got spit out of a machine under the counter. She took my suitcase. When she did, Mickey asked me, "Should I give her these?" meaning the bag from Rudolpho's and his bucket of quarters.

"No, you can carry them onto the plane."

Then the girl was handing me the tickets, saying, "Go directly to the gate. You have ten minutes. You should make it, but no stops."

"Got it."

We hurried down to the metal detector. I kept looking around to make sure no one was waiting for us. I knew we'd be fine once we got through the detector because it would hard for Doves' guys to get a gun through. That was proven by the fact that the detector beeped when I went through. I had to take off my belt and then my holster in order to get through.

"Where's the gun that goes with this?" the security guy asked.

"In my suitcase."

"Unloaded in a safety case?"

"Absolutely," I lied. It really wasn't the time for me to be truthful.

Then the security guy looked at Mickey's plastic bucket of quarters and simply rolled his eyes. After that, we ran to our gate. We were still walking down to our seats when they closed the doors behind us. I breathed a sigh of relief. Now all I had to do was worry about what was going to happen when we got off the plane at O'Hare.

The flight back was uneventful. I gave some thought to initiating Mickey into the mile high club—had even slipped a condom into my back pocket just in case—but he fell asleep as soon as the plane reached altitude. I wasn't as scared as I'd been on the flight out. I suppose being shot at would have that effect. About forty-five minutes into the flight I fell asleep and didn't wake until we were descending.

Mickey was already awake. He looked over at me and said, "Really gross, man."

That's when I realized I'd drooled down my chest. Great. Outside the sun was starting to rise. My Swatch said it was six-ten. We might be a bit earlier than I'd told Owen, but not by much. It seemed to take forever for them to let us off the plane, but when they finally did we walked out of gate H4 into terminal three. We followed the signs to baggage claim and got there quickly.

Baggage claim at O'Hare was bigger than it was in Vegas. All the conveyor belts lined up next to each other reminded me of a bowling alley. I looked around; there were people everywhere. More than there had been when I'd flown out of the airport. Near the luggage carousel, there was a big, round support holding up the building. I told Mickey to stand next to it and stay where I could see him. Standing there, scanning the low wide terminal, I didn't see anyone I recognized. I decided to page Owen. I might not call him back, but at least he'd know we'd landed.

Finally, the baggage for our flight started to come out. I kept scanning the area for Doves' guys and then I'd scan the conveyor belt for my suitcase. I hated that my new gun was still in the suitcase. Even thinking that made me worry that they'd pulled my bag aside because of the gun. They hadn't though. It finally came out and I stepped up to the carousel and grabbed it. Then I hurried back to Mickey and said, "Okay, let's go."

After an anxious two minutes, we got a cab. One of the newer Checker Cabs, a Chevy Impala painted the classic pale green and yellow. The driver wanted to put my bag in the trunk, but I waved him off. As we pulled away from the curb, I said to Mickey, "I miss Checker Cabs."

"This is a Checker Cab."

"I mean the real ones. This is just a Chevy."

He looked at me confused. I just smiled. I'd assumed he knew something about cars because of the way he doted on the Camaro. I was wrong. He knew about stripes and mag wheels, but not about cars.

As subtly as possible, I slipped my gun out of the suitcase and placed it into my shoulder holster. When I was sure that the driver wasn't going to freak and throw us out of the cab, I asked Mickey, "Nervous?"

"Yeah. Is Jimmy's lawyer gonna tell me what to say? Is that why we're going early?"

"Um, I think you're going to tell the truth. Devlin beat you up, didn't he?"

"Yeah, he did. But..."

"But what?"

"The things I told Devlin, they were all true. I don't wanna say that."

"I don't think it matters, Mickey. When a policeman beats a confession out of someone it doesn't matter if the confession is true or not."

"It matters that I told. That's what people are gonna remember."

"I think you did a smart thing going to Jimmy. I think if you help him out he'll help you out." Or at least I hoped so.

I had the driver take us down the Kennedy toward the Loop and then cut down to the Dan Ryan. We'd have to take the Stevenson back west a bit, but it seemed the smartest way to go. That is until we got to Addison. Traffic slowed to a crawl and I realized I hadn't taken the

Monday morning commute into consideration in any of my calculations. It was fine, I told myself; we were early.

"Are there gonna be a lot of people?"

"The courtroom's not that big, but it's been full every day."

I realized then that he was still carrying the Rudolpho's bag and hadn't changed into the clothes we bought.

"You want to change your clothes?"

"Here?"

"Sure why not? He's not going to throw us out on the Kennedy."

"I'm not...you know."

It took me a moment, then I went, "Oh." He wasn't wearing any underwear. He only had the one pair with him and those were in my suitcase waiting to be laundered. He could have washed them in the sink, or he could have borrowed a pair of mine. Both options were rejected in favor of not wearing any. "We'll find a men's room as soon as we get to the courthouse." I didn't think the cabbie would throw us out if Mickey changed his clothes, but if his dick was flopping around on the vinyl seat he just might.

I sat back and watched the city move by at a crawl. When we got to Fullerton, I considered having the cabbie, get off and cut down Western, but there was no guarantee we'd be better off.

My beeper went off and I looked at it. It was Owen's office number, so he'd gotten my page. I'd try giving him a call when we got to the courthouse, but he might already be there.

"This will all be over in a few hours," I said, as much to myself as to Mickey.

"And then what? I don't have my car; I don't have my fiancée. Everything sucks."

I considered pointing out the fact that he was still alive should go in the plus column, but he didn't seem to be in a space where he could hear that. The best I could come up with was, "Everything sucks until it doesn't."

He looked at me like I was a mental midget.

I kept my mouth shut for the next twenty minutes until we were finally getting off the Stevenson at Damen.

"We're gonna go right in, right through the metal detectors and up to the courtroom. Jimmy's attorneys will either already be there or they're on their way. We'll get you changed, then they'll probably have some advice for you about what to say."

"You told me to tell the truth."

"And they're going to tell you *how* to tell the truth."

"There's only one way to tell the truth." Mickey would not have made a good lawyer.

"They can't ask you directly about Captain Devlin. They can't ask you directly if he beat you to get you to confess. You can talk about Devlin in your answers though. You can talk about what happened. When you do, though, the state's attorney will make a lot of noise. They want to keep all of that from the jury. And the judge has gone along to a certain extent."

"That doesn't make any sense."

"It will when the lawyers go over it," I said, hoping I was right. Also hoping none of what I'd said could be construed as witness tampering.

As soon as the cab got to the corner of 26th and Cal we were jockeying for position. Even though it was still early, there was a line of cabs in front of us, a couple of limousines and dozens of people on the sidewalk flowing up the steps to the courthouse. I threw some money at our cabbie and we jumped out. Cutting through the double-parked cars, we hurried up across the sidewalk and then started up the steps. Then something hit me. My gun was in its holster. I needed to walk through a metal detector. But I couldn't. Not with my gun underneath my arm.

So what did I do with it? Shit, I wasn't thinking. I used to have a carry permit but it was expired and I didn't even have that with me. I had my PI license, so I could do a song and dance about having forgotten my carry permit, but they'd probably take it away from and since it was unregistered I'd be unlikely to get it back.

"Look, Mickey, you need to go ahead. I have to take care of something."

"What? No. I can't go in there alone."

"I'll be right there. Just go."

I hurried back down the steps. It took just a moment to pick out a cab that was letting off an older man in an expensive suit. Before he could shut the door, I stuck my head in and offered the driver thirty bucks to take my bag home for me. Even before he agreed, I was opening the suitcase and slipping my gun inside. The driver saw what I was doing and said, "Forty."

"Sure, forty." Of course, there was nothing to stop him from driving off with my suitcase, my gun and my forty bucks, so I told him there'd be another twenty when it arrived. I'd need to call Joseph and tell him I kept some extra cash in my copy of Stephen King's *The Stand*.

"Okay. Great."

I gave him my address and two twenties. Just to be extra sure, I took a glance at his license taped to the glove box. His name was Sabbir—

At first, I thought it was a car backfiring, but then I realized it was a shot because it was followed almost immediately by the sound of breaking glass. Then there were two more shots. I pulled my head out of the cab and saw that people were running every which way. I looked up the courthouse steps. At the top, someone was down. I saw a pair of jeans, a bit of black T-shirt. Quarters were bouncing down the steps. The Rudolpho's bag was lying a few steps from the top. I ran up the steps as quickly as I could. My stomach trying to jump out of my body. Mickey was there on the top step. A dark, wet spot was spreading in the T-shirt making the graphic harder to see. I was down on my knees next to him. The bullet seemed to have gone into this stomach dead center. I pressed down on the wound. I could feel the beating of his heart in my palms.

"What happened? Where did the shot come from?"

"I don't know. I heard the first shot and turned around. I was trying to see what was going on. It didn't hurt. I just kind of fell down."

The blood wasn't stopping. I took my jacket off, folded it, and pressed it into Mickey's belly. Then I looked around, yelling, "Ten-one" over and over. Stupid, I know. I hadn't been on the job for six years.

"Okay, that hurts," Mickey said, interrupting me.

"Why? Why didn't you do what I told you?"

"I didn't know where to go."

I almost screamed, "Inside," but I didn't want to make this any worse than it was. "I'm sorry, I should have been more specific."

And then, finally, officers came out the courthouse. As soon as I saw one I yelled, "Hey! We need an ambulance."

"What happened?"

"Someone shot him."

"Were they on foot or in a car?"

"I don't know. I was down at the curb looking the other way."

The officer looked at Mickey and asked, "What about you, sir? Did you see anything?"

Mickey shook his head.

I could have been annoyed that he didn't run off and call an ambulance right away, but I knew better. First, determine if the shooter is in the area. When the scene is secure, take care of the wounded. He had a walkie-talkie clipped to his belt. He pulled it off and called for an ambulance. Someone inside must have beaten him to the punch, though, because seconds later an ambulance arrived, as did a half dozen squads all blocking the street.

Chaos broke out like a rash. The EMTs pushed me out of the way so they could get to Mickey. They barked a few things at each other and then got him on a long backboard. I asked if I could go in the ambulance but was told no. I did get them to tell me they were taking him, to St. Tony's. They started to carry Mickey down the steps. I was going to go with him at least to the back of the ambulance, but a couple of detectives were on me.

Cheap suits, comb-overs, one of them actually chewing on a cigar. They were from the ninth or tenth district, I didn't catch all of what they were saying. They had names, but I was too busy trying to remember my own to remember theirs.

"Who are you?"

"Nick Nowak."

"What are you doing here?"

"You on trial for something?"

"I'm a private investigator working the Jimmy English trial. The guy in the ambulance is Mickey Troccoli, a witness scheduled to testify this morning." More than he asked, but he'd get around to the questions that went with my answers eventually.

"So you know who shot your friend?" the cigar-chomper asked.

"I was down at the curb paying a cabbie." That was marginally true. "I didn't see anything."

"Jimmy English. That's what you just said, huh?"

"Yeah, that's what I just said."

"In other words, it's a good idea not to see anything," that was the cigar-chomper again. I was starting to dislike him.

"Yeah. It's safer that way," the other one chimed in.

"I really didn't see anything, okay? I was supposed to be protecting him."

The ambulance popped its siren on and sped away. For the first time, I wondered if Mickey was going to make it. Was he going to live? He had to make it. I didn't want this on my—

"Where's the gun that goes in that holster?" Cigar reached out and touched my shoulder holster. I took a step back. I didn't like him touching me.

"In Las Vegas."

"Really?"

"It's illegal to have guns in Chicago."

"That doesn't mean people don't have 'em."

I'd had about enough of this. "You know I don't have to talk to you if I don't want to. And I don't want to."

"Explain something to me," the cigar-chomper said, "What exactly was you gonna do if you'd been standing right next to this Troccoli kid? You ain't got a gun. Was you gonna throw yourself in front of a bullet?"

He was poking at me but I couldn't help answering. "There were three shots. The first one missed. I heard breaking glass. I could have pulled him down."

"Newsflash, people get shot on the ground, too."

"Great, you convinced me. I didn't do anything wrong." They hadn't. I just wanted to get away from them.

"Oh, we think you did something wrong. It just ain't what you're saying it is." I wanted to shove the cigar down his throat.

"You want to know who wanted Mickey Troccoli dead? ASA Sanchez. Go talk to her. Because I'm finished."

I turned and walked away. But I had no idea where I was going.

Chapter Seventeen

I walked through the metal detector without being stopped. No one was there. Everyone was on the steps in front of the courthouse. Blindly, I walked across the lobby heading to the payphones I'd used just a few days before to call Nello Mosby's friends. It seemed like a very long time ago. People stared at me. I looked down at my clothes and saw that I was covered in blood. Huh, that was so weird. My clothes looked like Nello's.

At the payphones, I set my rolled up jacket on the counter and dug a quarter out of my jeans, dumped it into the phone and dialed. A couple rings later, Joseph answered.

"Hi."

"Oh my God, Nick! We were watching Geraldine Ferraro on Phil Donahue and they interrupted to talk about a shooting at the courthouse. We saw you. We saw you all covered in blood."

I had no idea there had been TV cameras; couldn't remember seeing them.

"What time is it?" I hadn't wanted to reach into my blood soaked jacket to get the Swatch.

"It's like ten minutes after nine. Tell me you're okay."

"I'm okay."

"Good. I mean, we thought you were. You were moving around, so we thought you were okay. Oh Nick, I'm so sorry. Did the guy die?"

"No. Not yet at least."

"They said you threw yourself on the victim to protect him."

"That's not true. The shooting was over before I got to him. All I did was try to stop the bleeding." And not very well judging by my clothes. "Did they use my name?"

"Not unless you changed it to Unidentified Man."

"Okay, good." Publicity was not my thing. "Did they use Mickey's name?"

"No. The just said he was a witness in a drug case."

Normally, that was a safe bet. Most of what happened at the courthouse had to do with drugs. Jimmy's was one of the few trials not connected to drugs.

"Hold on," Joseph said. "Someone's at the door."

I heard him talking into the intercom, then he came back to the phone. "There's a cab downstairs. Says he has a suitcase?"

"Yeah. Do you have twenty bucks?"

"Uh-huh."

"Good. Give him twenty bucks and I'll pay you back later."

"Okay. Here, talk to Ross. I'll be right back."

There was a little static as he handed the phone off to Ross.

"Did you get shot at?" Ross asked.

"Yeah. Twice. Don't tell Joseph. He thinks it was only once." I'd decide whether to tell him about Friday night later on.

"He was worried. We haven't heard from you since Friday. *We* were worried."

"Sorry. We were kind of hiding out. I can't talk about this shit anymore. Tell me what you guys did this weekend."

"Joseph got you a costume for Brian's party Wednesday."

"Wednesday? Is it already Halloween?"

"In two days."

"I don't wear costumes. Did you tell him that?"

"You'll wear this one."

"I probably won't." I probably would. I just hoped that resisting would allow me some leeway. I had no desire to go anywhere dressed as E.T. or Tarzan. "What else happened this weekend? Is Joseph feeling better?"

"Oh, yeah, he's all better."

"Good."

"I walked over to Brian's for dinner Saturday night."

I was tempted to ask where Joseph was, but I knew better. He was doing whatever he was doing. Just like I was. That was the deal.

"Are you going to be okay?" he asked, concerned.

"What do you mean? I'm fine."

"Nick."

"I'm fine. I am."

"Here's Joseph."

"Okay. Your suitcase is here."

"Good. Inside there's a small handgun. It's loaded so be careful. I'm pretty sure the safety is on but still...be careful. Take it and the extra ammunition to Brian's."

"Why? Did you do something?"

"No. But I don't want anyone taking it away from me."

"Okay." He sounded doubtful.

"Don't worry. Everything's fine."

"When are you coming home?"

"I don't know. I haven't been up to the courtroom yet. I don't know how this is going to change things. Mickey was supposed to testify at ten o'clock."

"So whoever didn't want him to testify succeeded."

"That they did."

When I hung up, I realized that I'd gotten blood all over the receiver. My hands were still covered in Mickey's blood. The men's room was right there. Inside, I went right for a sink, dumping my jacket into the one next to me, and started to wash my hands. It's not easy washing off blood. Just ask Lady Macbeth.

After a few minutes, I looked up and saw that not only was there blood all over my yellow and blue checked shirt, there were spatters on my face and neck. I pulled the shirt away from my skin. It was beginning to clot. I picked up my jacket, opening it up. It was a checkerboard of bloodstains. It was obviously ruined. I'd never wear it again. That made me sad. And then it made me feel like an asshole. Mickey was at St. Tony's maybe dying and I was feeling sad about a corduroy jacket. That made me the definition of an asshole.

I thought about trying to clean myself up some more, but it was overwhelming. All I really wanted to do was get into a cab, go home, strip off my clothes, throw them all away and take a weeklong shower. But I still had to find Owen. I took the Swatch out and wiped the blood off its face. It was a quarter after nine. How did that happen? Where did the time go to? How long had I been in the men's room? The morning had a surreal, disconnected feeling that wasn't likely to go away anytime soon. I left the restroom and took the elevator to the sixth floor.

When I walked into the courtroom, Owen saw me right away. He hurried over in the gallery. "Where have you been? Where is Mickey? Oh my God, you're covered—"

"Where the fuck have you been? You were supposed to meet us."

"I was running late and when I got here it was almost impossible to get near—oh shit. That was Mickey? People said one of the cops got shot."

"No. Not even close."

Then Babcock was there, "What is happening? Where is our witness?" He saw the blood on my shirt and recoiled. "Is he dead?"

"He's at St. Tony's."

"St. Tony's? Is that a pizza place?"

"St. Anthony's. Hospital." I'm sure Nathan Babcock thought the only hospital in Chicago was Northwestern.

"When is he getting out?"

"He has a gunshot wound. It could be a while. Or it could be never."

Immediately, Babcock and Owen huddled to talk about what this meant to the trial. Then the bailiff announced the judge and everyone stood up. The judge was early and the jury had not been brought in yet. Presumably, Judge Corbin wanted to get a sense of what direction things were going and deal with any motions before he let them in.

Babcock and Owen turned and moved down the aisle, I followed after them. Jimmy sat at the defense table, holding the top of his cane with one hand. Something fluttered across his face when he saw me, I couldn't tell if it was regret or anger. ASA Sanchez's face was more readable. She looked at me with great disdain, as though I'd committed an unpardonable social sin. Unexpectedly, I heard Judge Corbin say, "Young man, how dare you come into my courtroom like that?"

I was speechless for a moment, then stuttered out "This is Mickey Troccoli's blood."

Judge Corbin chewed on that for only a moment.

"Is he dead?"

"Not yet."

"Is he going to live?"

"He might."

"Then I think we should move on to our next witness."

"What?" ASA Sanchez practically yelled. "Your honor!"

"Ms. Sanchez. I was not inclined to grant your motion. And now that we know our witness is alive and may be available in a few days, there's even more reason not to have his prior statements read into the record."

"Yes, but it would really be better for the jury's understanding of the case to hear what Mr. Troccoli said—"

"A witness in this trial was shot on the courthouse steps. I'm going to have to sequester the jury immediately. I'm not going to keep them away from their families and their lives any longer than need be. We're proceeding and we're proceeding today. Unless you prefer that I declare a mistrial?"

Briefly, she seemed to calculate the positive or negative effect of a mistrial on her career. "No, your honor, I would not like you to declare a mistrial."

"In that case, we should bring in the jury."

"Your honor?"

"What now, Ms. Sanchez?"

"The state asks that Mr. Nowak be removed from the courtroom. His appearance is prejudicial. Not to mention confusing."

Babcock was standing. "Your honor, Mr. Nowak is intimately versed in the prior statements of all witnesses. It would be a significant disadvantage not to have him present." It was sort of true.

"How long do you need?"

Babcock bent over and consulted with Owen. "An hour?"

"We will reconvene in an hour."

Then he left the courtroom, people shuffled around. Owen came over and I said, "I guess I should go buy some clothes." The Rudolpho's bag crossed my mind. Where had it ended up? I could have worn those clothes. They would have been too small but I'd have been covered. Well, mostly covered.

"No, not you," Owen said. Then he turned to the ever silent Mrs. Barnes. "Take a cab to Field's and get Nick a pair of jeans and a dress shirt."

I started to give her my sizes but she stopped me. "I know your sizes. I have two boys twenty-three and twenty-five. They're both about your height." It was the first and only thing she'd said to me. She hurried off.

"Come on," Owen said. "We should get you cleaned up."

"I did…"

"No dear, you didn't."

I followed him out of the courtroom and down the hallway. The restroom was high-ceiling, narrow and covered in dingy white marble. The fixtures were heavy porcelain and stained in rust. The stalls didn't have doors; the only one I could see into was missing a toilet, too. In a corner, the ceiling dripped in a steady stream. The place was in horrible disrepair; apparently, the county didn't think lawyers and criminals worth spending money on.

Owen led me over to a sink and said, "Take your shirt off."

Numbly, I did as I was told. He pulled a half dozen paper towels out of the one working dispenser, wet them and began wiping blood off my chest.

"Who's the next witness?" I asked.

"Nino Nitti, Jr. But... Sanchez could take this opportunity to change directions. Her original strategy was to begin with the smaller charges then work her way up to murder. She'd then use Jimmy's family and the journal to tie Jimmy to the crimes."

"But you think she'll abandon that?"

"Without Mickey or his testimony she can't connect Jimmy. If she's smart she'll switch to Jimmy's family, use the journal to connect Jimmy to the crimes, and then go back and outline the murders. My God, there's even blood in your hair."

I decided not to think about that. "Meanwhile Sanchez hopes that Mickey dies."

"Well, yes, that would be convenient for her. Failing that, she'll put him on the stand and ask just one question."

"One?"

"Yes. 'Have you ever received money from Giovanni Agnotti?'"

"If he says yes, then she's connected him to Jimmy," I supplied. Owen rubbed my head with wet paper towels. "And if he says no?"

"She asks the judge to instruct him on the meaning of perjury. And asks again. If he continues to say no she'll ask if he told a CPD officer that he worked for Jimmy." Owen threw away a bunch of paper towels. "You should take your pants off."

I took my pants off. That left me standing in my boxers, which were blood-tinged around the waistband. "But isn't that what Sanchez wants to avoid. Talking about Mickey's interview."

"Yes, of course. But by asking only the one question, she'd limit the scope of our cross. She'd also object to virtually everything we asked based on the exclusion of Devlin."

"You could bring Mickey back as a defense witness."

"True. But if it appears the sole reason to do so is to allow Mickey to volunteer information about Devlin, the judge will likely shut it down. In fact, Sanchez would probably bring that up in a sidebar before the testimony even began, so if we even got close—"

The restroom door opened and Tony Stork walked in. He gave my near nudity the once over in a way that made me want to put my bloody clothes back on. He walked over to one of the urinals and unzipped his trousers.

"Too bad about your witness."

"Your witness," I pointed out.

"Yes, that's true. Kind of you to bring him back for us."

"I do what I can."

I looked at Owen, who raised an eyebrow. Tony finished pissing, then pushed his hips back to make it appear he was putting away a monster dick. If I recalled correctly, it wasn't. He walked over to the sink right next to us and washed his hands. As he dried his hands he gave me the once over again and said, "You've lost weight."

I glared at him as he walked out of the men's room.

"Why do I think there's a story there?" Owen asked.

"It's not important. Look, Owen, I know that diary is a fake. I figured that out weeks ago."

"Did you? Well, I'm not surprised."

"Would you like to explain why one of the State's main pieces of evidence is fake?"

"No. I wouldn't, actually. In fact, I can't."

"This is all about Deanna Hansen, isn't it? Her grandfather tried to breakup her relationship with Turi Bova and she wouldn't have it."

"That's an interesting theory."

Which told me I was completely wrong.

Chapter Eighteen

"Your honor, we'd like to call Rosa Hansen to the stand," Tony Stork stood up and said, then waited for a complaint from the defense. It didn't come.

I was back in my seat next to Mrs. Barnes wearing a pair of sharply creased blue slacks, a light blue oxford shirt, and navy tie with white dots. It all fit and it all felt wrong. Across from me, the jury had been seated. They looked sullen and miserable, so they'd obviously been told they were going to be sequestered.

The courtroom seemed to contain more people than it had before; it didn't, it just seemed that way. I glanced through the gallery and noticed that the two guys I was sure worked for Doves, the guys I was sure were in the Lincoln Continental in Vegas, the guys who at the very least arranged for Mickey to get shot, were not there.

Jimmy's daughter made her way from the gallery to the witness stand. She looked completely at ease in a stiff, sharply tailored charcoal-colored suit. Taking her seat, she crossed her legs and looked at Tony with disdain.

"Mrs. Hansen, your birth name is Rosa Agnotti?"

"It is. I don't use that name though. I prefer to be called Rose. Rose Hansen."

"And Giovanni Agnotti is your father?"

"He is."

"Do you have any knowledge of the crimes your father has been accused of?"

"Of course not."

Tony looked down at his notes.

"Is that it? Can I go?" Rose asked hopefully.

"I'm sorry," Tony said. "Just needed to check my notes. Ms. Agnotti—"

"Mrs. Hansen."

Tony smiled at her in a way that told the jury she was hostile.

"When you were a child, in grade school, what kind of notebook did you use?"

"What?"

"Notebook. For your classes."

"I don't know. I don't remember."

Tony flipped open his briefcase and took out an obviously aged red notebook with an Indian Chief on the cover. The notebook was in a large plastic bag with a label stuck to it. "Your honor, I'd like to enter this into evidence. State's exhibit four.

Tony brought the notebook to the bench and handed it to Judge Corbin. Corbin glanced at it and then at the defense table.

"The defense has already been provided with a Xerox copy of the notebook," Tony answered the obvious question.

Corbin handed the notebook back to Tony.

For the benefit of the court reporter, Tony said, "Now I'm showing the exhibit to the witness. Mrs. Hansen. This is a Big Chief Tablet purchased for ten cents. Do you recognize it?"

Rose frowned and tried to form an answer. "I

recognize that kind of tablet. I can't say if I recognize that...particular tablet. Does it have my algebra notes in it?"

This earned a soft chuckle from the gallery.

"Given your comment, I assume this is the kind of notebook you used in grade school?"

"I might have. I think I used different kinds."

"Did you purchase your own school supplies?"

"No. Usually my mother did."

"Usually? If your mother didn't purchase the notebook, who did?"

"The maid."

"Did your father ever purchase school supplies for you?"

"He doesn't like shopping. The only thing I remember my father buying for himself was a Cadillac."

Another chuckle bounced around the courtroom. Jimmy leaned over and said something to Nathan Babcock.

"Is it possible that your mother, or the maid, might have given your father a notebook like this?"

Rose looked at the defense table. The question so clearly asked her to guess it deserved an objection. But one was not forthcoming. Babcock sat stony-still waiting for her to answer.

"I don't have any direct knowledge of that."

"I didn't ask that. I asked if it was possible."

"You're asking me to guess."

"Yes, please, guess."

"I guess someone could have given my father that sort of notebook."

"You have no knowledge of you father keeping a diary or journal?"

"Why would he do something like that?"

"Does that mean no?"

"I don't recall my father keeping a diary."

"But then, you wouldn't, would you?"

Rose looked confused a moment, then said, "I can't know what I don't know."

"Your father kept his criminal activities separate from his home life."

"My father has never been convicted of a crime. He kept his *business* life separate from his home life, that is true."

"I stand corrected," Tony said tartly. "You father could have kept a *business* diary and you wouldn't have known."

Again Rose looked over at Babcock and nothing happened. This time she looked at the judge, as well. Then she said in disgust, "This is nothing more than a guessing game."

I wasn't sure why Babcock wasn't objecting, but her comment was more persuasive than a dozen objections. The judge finally intervened. "Mr. Stork, perhaps you could ask the witness about things she actually knows."

"Thank you, your honor," Rose said.

Tony opened the plastic bag and took out the notebook. He opened it and held it in front of Rose. "Is this your father's handwriting?"

With a shrug, Rose said, "I don't know."

"You don't know if it's your father's handwriting?"

"That's what I said."

"But Mrs. Hansen, you would recognize your father's handwriting, wouldn't you?"

"No. I wouldn't. We don't correspond. We live twenty minutes apart. We talk on the telephone."

"Your father has never written you a birthday card?"

"My mother did that."

"Are you saying you've never seen your father's handwriting?"

She considered a bit, then, "I can't say I've never seen it. I may have. But I wouldn't recognize it. That was your question, wasn't it?"

Tony had to take another look at his notes. This was not going as well as he'd hoped. I was pretty sure he was trying to get Rose to authenticate the notebook, but she'd just failed to do so.

"So you're saying that you've never seen your father's handwriting and you've never seen this notebook." He said it with as much contempt as he could muster, attempting, I assume, to make her seem a liar.

Rose didn't answer. Finally, reluctantly, she said, "I have. I have seen the notebook before."

Everything got very quiet for a moment, then Tony pounced, "So you did see the notebook around the house when you were a child?"

"No. My daughter showed it to me about a year ago."

That was huge. Rose had never said anything like that before, either in interviews with the task force or with Owen. I was tempted to lean forward, tap him on the shoulder and remind him of that, but I was fairly certain he already knew. Meanwhile, Tony was pulled into a whispered conversation with ASA Sanchez. They had a difficult decision to make. Rose was on the verge of impeaching their witness before they even put her on the stand.

Suddenly, Sanchez stood and said, "We have no further questions for this witness."

Judge Corbin looked at the defense table. Babcock stood up and said, "Good Morning, Mrs. Hansen. I don't think this will take much longer."

Rose smiled at him.

"Why don't we start with your daughter, Deanna, showing you the notebook the State says belonged to your father. Can you tell us about that?"

"Objection," Sanchez said. "Response requires narrative."

"Sustained."

"When your daughter showed you the notebook in question, what did she say?"

"She said she'd stolen it from my father's office."

"His place of business?"

"Yes."

Jimmy had told me the book was stolen from his home. That he'd fired his staff because of it. But then he'd also told me he kept the diary. I didn't know what was true and what wasn't, but I did know the story kept changing.

"Did she say exactly where she'd taken it from?"

"There's a safe, apparently."

"Did she say how she got into the safe?"

"My father gave her the combination."

"So it's not exactly theft."

"Objection. Testifying."

"I'll withdraw. Did she say why she took the notebook?"

"She said she wanted to hurt him. Her grandfather."

"Now, when she showed you the notebook what were your thoughts?"

"Objection. Vague."

"Did you think the notebook was real?"

"Objection. Calls for speculation."

"Oh really?" Babcock said. "I seem to recall the state asking a number of speculative questions to which we didn't object. I think we should be allowed some leeway."

I gasped a little. Loud enough for Owen to turn around and look at me. Babcock had known Rose would say Deanna had shown her the notebook. He'd let her speculate for the State so that he could ask for the same courtesy. He knew exactly where this was all going.

Judge Corbin eyed ASA Sanchez. "He has a point, Ms. Sanchez. I'll allow. Once."

"Do you think the notebook was created by your father? Giovanni Agnotti?"

"No. I do not."

"Did you tell your daughter that?"

"Of course."

"And her response was?"

"That it didn't matter. That she could hurt him with it anyway."

"Thank you. I have no more questions."

Judge Corbin asked if the state would like to redirect. Sanchez stood and said, "Yes, your honor, we would. Mrs. Hansen, do you know that your father did *not* write the journal your daughter showed you?"

"No. I don't."

"No further questions."

There was a pause while Rose left the witness stand and went to sit down. ASA Sanchez shuffled a few papers around. Sanchez had stepped all over Tony Stork's toes by stealing his witness. I doubted he'd be given much chance to squeal about it though. Someone was going to have to take the blame for Rose's revelations and it would probably be Tony.

ASA Sanchez took a deep breath and said, "The State would like to call Deanna Hansen."

Deanna stood up in the gallery and came to the aisle. She didn't look at her mother or at her grandfather. She walked to the witness stand with her eyes forward and her face placid. She wore a red wraparound dress with cap sleeves and a large white lapel. It was too old for her and completely wrong for court. She looked a bit like a teenager playing dress-up. It had to be deliberate. She was too smart for it not to be. If she looked inappropriate it was because she wanted to look inappropriate.

"Good morning, Ms. Hansen." Sanchez's voice was chilly. I think she'd realized that there was no telling what Deanna might say.

"Good morning."

"For the record, Giovanni Agnotti is your grandfather and Rosa Agnotti Hansen is your mother."

"Yes."

"Do you have a good relationship with your grandfather?"

"Most of the time."

"Do you have a good relationship with your mother?"

"Some of the time."

"We've been discussing a notebook. Are you familiar with it?"

"Yes."

Sanchez held up the notebook so that Deanna could see it clearly. "And you gave *this* notebook to the task force investigating your grandfather."

"I did."

"You told them your grandfather kept the notebook."

"I did."

"In addition to giving them your grandfather's notebook, you told them a number of stories that your grandfather shared with you."

"I did."

"You related a story in which your grandfather admitted his involvement in the deaths of Shady and Josette Perrelli."

Deanna nodded.

"You have to actually answer," Sanchez said.

Annoyance crept into her voice. I was sure she'd already explained this to Deanna.

"Yes, I did tell them that."

To me, Sanchez seemed to be skipping all over the place, but when she returned to the very beginning I realized that she'd been sketching out the testimony she wanted to cover and now she wanted to get into the details. Holding up the Big Chief notebook again, she asked, "Can you tell us how the notebook came into your possession?"

"I took it from my grandparents' home."

"Your grandparents' home? Not your grandfather's office?"

"No."

"So your mother was wrong?"

Sanchez was hoping for a "yes," as it would serve to lessen Rose's believability. She was disappointed.

"I did tell my mother I took the notebook from my grandfather's safe."

"I see." Sanchez seemed to struggle with whether to ask why. Like most lawyers, she liked to know the answer to the questions she asked. She moved on. "Where in your grandparents' home did you find the notebook?"

"It was in my grandfather's study. On his desk."

"And when did you find the notebook?"

"I was about ten, I think. That would make it sometime in nineteen seventy-three."

Sanchez gave Deanna a look that said, 'I want to come over there and stab you with a pencil.' Instead, she collected herself and said, "Ms. Hansen, you know that you're under oath?"

"Yes, I understand that. It was sometime in nineteen seventy-three. I'm sorry I can't be more specific. It was a long time ago."

"Let me make sure I understand you. You first found the notebook when you were ten. Your grandfather was recording his activities in the book. And then last year—"

"Objection, leading the witness."

"Sorry, your honor. Let me try again. When you found the book in nineteen seventy-three, how many of the pages were taken up with your grandfather's entries?"

"None. The book was empty."

"You told the task force you took the notebook from your grandfather's home just last year?"

"I did. That was a lie."

"There are federal agents on the task force. Lying to a federal agent is a crime."

"Is that something Captain Devlin should have mentioned when he was beating up my boyfriend?"

There was a generalized grumbling around the courtroom. Everyone seemed to want to comment to a friend about what she'd just said. ASA Sanchez turned her back on Deanna as though to invalidate her, and said, "Move to strike, your honor. Testimony about Captain Devlin has been excluded."

"This is your witness, Ms. Sanchez. The exclusion prevents the defense from calling Captain Devlin to the stand or calling witnesses to discuss Captain Devlin. It does not prevent your witness from invoking his name."

"In that case, your honor, please remind the witness that she's under oath and outline the penalties for perjury so she fully understands them."

"Do you understand what perjury is Ms. Hansen?" the Judge asked.

"Your honor, I'm in law school."

"The witness understands the concept of perjury. Please continue Ms. Sanchez."

"If we could have just a moment."

"Take two," Judge Corbin suggested.

Sanchez and Stork had a whispered conference. It was hard to tell if they were talking strategy or if Sanchez was trying to turn the reins over to Stork so she could flee the sinking ship. They were obviously in a bad place. It wasn't safe to continue asking Deanna questions, but it was more dangerous to turn her over to cross.

Abruptly, Babcock stood. "Your honor, the State has failed to make their case. We ask for a directed verdict."

"No. Your honor—"

Judge Corbin held up a hand to silence Sanchez. "Mr. Babcock, I understand we may be moving in that direction, however, I'm not there yet. I'd like to hear more from the witness about this notebook and how it came to be given to the task force. And I'm sure the jury would, too." We'd almost completely forgotten the jury. They looked around in surprise at being mentioned.

Sanchez looked at the judge like she wanted to chew off her own tongue rather than ask another question, but she went ahead, "Tell the judge about the notebook."

"I took it from my grandfather's house when I was ten. I liked to draw horses at the time. I only used the first few pages. If you look closely at the notebook, you'll see that the first five or six pages have been torn out. Then I stuck it in a drawer and forgot about it." Deanna took a breath and continued. "When Devlin wanted me to come up with some evidence against my grandfather I tore the pages out that I'd drawn on and wrote out the diary based on what Devlin wanted. He was very specific about the phrase 'N took care of the Ps' on October 12, 1973."

"You really expect us to believe that you faked your grandfather's journal and then no one on the task force noticed," Sanchez briefly flared back to life.

"Well…I don't know who else on the task force knew

about the notebook. I mean they could all—"

"All right," Sanchez said stopping Deanna. "Your honor, I can assure you that no one in my office was aware of Ms. Hansen's fraud."

"And this is your primary bit of evidence?" the judge asked.

"And the stories Ms. Hansen—" She stopped, realizing those were likely to be lies as well. "We have Nino Nitti, Jr. it was his father who—"

"Was he interviewed by Captain Devlin?"

"Yes."

"I'm afraid I'm going to have to entertain Mr. Babcock's motion for a directed verdict."

"Mistrial," Sanchez quickly said. "I motion for a mistrial."

"The defense strenuously objects to a mistrial."

I was struggling to keep up. I was pretty sure a directed verdict and a mistrial would both result in Jimmy's walking free. The only real difference I could see was that a directed verdict would be a loss for Sanchez, while a mistrial would be more of a draw.

Judge Corbin sighed heavily. I could see him adding everything up. A witness shot on the courthouse steps and currently in the hospital. Every single witness tainted by police misconduct. Witnesses who either lied to federal agents or were perjuring themselves. It was a mess. A big mess.

"Ms. Sanchez, you indicted Mr. Agnotti on a smorgasbord of charges and yet there isn't enough real evidence here to convict him of jaywalking. I could grant you a mistrial, but my fear is you'll be back in court with the same list of charges and just as little evidence. Not to mention, if you did come up with any real evidence against Mr. Agnotti it's now so tainted by what we've seen in this trial there would be no possibility of a conviction. Therefore I'm granting Mr. Babcock his directed verdict."

He banged the gavel and it was over.

Chapter Nineteen

The moment the gavel came down, the courtroom erupted into a chaotic frenzy far too similar to the one I'd experienced on the steps of the courthouse. People seemed to be going every which way. A half dozen people were congratulating Nathan Babcock on a job well done. Jimmy's family surrounded him: Rose, Deanna, Beverly, even Lydia was allowed to get close to the old man. Turi Bova hovered nearby.

In the pants that Mrs. Barnes had bought me, my beeper went off. My first thought was that it had something to do with the trial ending, but when I checked it, I didn't recognize the number. It was an 864 number. I didn't know where that was. Maybe for giggles, I'd call it later.

Over at the State's table, Sanchez and Tony Stork looked almost lonely as they gathered their things. I couldn't help myself, I walked over and addressed the top of ASA Sanchez's head, "I hope you're proud of yourself."

Looking up at me, she said, "Why would I be proud of myself? I just lost the most important case of my career." She didn't seem particularly put out.

"You got Mickey Troccoli shot. He might die."

Tony paled and his eyes widened. I imagine he thought I was making a big mistake.

"That seems like very creative thinking, Mr. Nowak."

"I remember what you said exactly. You said Mickey was a witness in another 'case of this nature.' You implied that Mickey was a witness in an investigation into Doves, knowing Doves had guys sitting in the gallery."

She tried not to know what I was talking about. "Oh, that. I'm afraid you're mistaken. I may have accidentally referred to our investigation of Captain Devlin...we're considering using Mickey Troccoli as a witness against him, you see."

"Don't play dumb. You never accidentally do anything."

"Compliments from the defense team. How unexpected."

"You knew exactly what you were doing. You knew everyone would assume that you were talking about Doves. You knew they'd have to do something about it."

"You can hardly hold me responsible for the assumptions other people make."

But I did. She knew what they'd assume and she knew what would happen. She'd done it deliberately. Mickey's blood was on her hands and she couldn't care less.

"Do you know that it was Doves who had Mickey shot? Get me evidence and I'll prosecute."

I think my jaw dropped. She didn't believe in good and evil. She didn't even believe in justice. She only believed in winning. And she didn't care how she did it.

She had her things packed up and without another word walked away from me. Tony trailed after her, but not before giving me a look that clearly said, "You crazy fool."

Suddenly, I was exhausted. Well, that was no surprise. I hadn't gotten much sleep in the last seventy-two hours. But it was more than physical. It was emotional. This whole thing with Jimmy was hitting me hard.

I sat down at the State's table because it was right there. I looked across at the defense. Deanna was helping her grandfather stand, her mother and aunt fluttering nearby. I'd been thinking this was a story of shifting alliances, that Deanna had been against Jimmy; that Mickey had been against him, too. But they weren't. There were no shifting alliances. They'd both always been with him.

In February I'd been hired to find out the identity of the informant the task force had dubbed Prince Charles. I'd found out Deanna was Prince Charles. Except she wasn't Prince Charles, she was a Trojan horse. She went in and gave the task force false evidence. Evidence that had just destroyed their case. Jimmy had known all along, presumably so had his attorneys. I was hired to find out something they already knew. Why?

I thought about it for a moment, shutting out the noise around me. When the answer came, it was simple. Jimmy wanted the task force to think he didn't know what he knew. The task force knew I was looking for Prince Charles—Devlin threatened me about it—that would convince them that Jimmy had no idea who was informing on him. It was all a con. Jimmy had been conning Operation Tea & Crumpets.

Wait. What about Devlin? The whole thing began with Devlin beating a confession out of Mickey Troccoli. So, Jimmy and Owen and Babcock, and just about everyone but me, knew exactly how dangerous Devlin was right from the start. That part wasn't okay with me. Well, none of it was okay with me when it came down to it.

Christian Baylor died because of Jimmy's con. So did a guy named Digby. So did a valet whose name I couldn't even remember. Part of the reason they all died was that I didn't know what was really going on. What did they die for? What was the point of Jimmy's con?

Babcock and Jimmy's family were leading the old man out of the courtroom. He looked fragile and burdened by all the help he was receiving. Owen was behind them talking on his brick-sized mobile phone. Hanging up, he smiled and walked over to me.

"Mickey's in surgery. They're optimistic."

That was a small glimmer at the bottom of what was turning into a large pile of shit.

"You used me."

"You were useful."

"You lied to me."

"It was my job to lie to you. You have noticed that I'm a lawyer haven't you?"

"I was part of the team. Confidentiality extended to me."

"Jimmy didn't want too many people to know."

"You still should have told me."

"Darling, I couldn't."

"He can't be tried again, can he?"

"No, of course not."

"Was that the whole point?"

"Nick, you need to forget about all of this. It's over."

"Did Jimmy have the Perellis killed?"

"I never ask clients questions like that. It makes it easier to sleep at night."

"I guess that's the most important thing. Whether you sleep at night."

"It's important to me." He glanced across the courtroom to watch as Jimmy was led out by his family.

"You should have congratulated Jimmy. I'm sure he wants to thank you for your hard work."

But I didn't want to congratulate him. I wanted to go home. I wanted to go to sleep.

"I'm done," I told Owen.

"Of course you are," he replied. "Darling, go home, get drunk, fuck your pretty boyfriend, get some sleep. Call me in a few days. I'm sure I can find other work for you."

"No. I'm done. I'm done with you."

"Oh, I see. You're taking this personally."

"Three people died. Mickey might still die. I was nearly killed."

"Yes, I understand. But none of that is Jimmy's fault. None of that is my fault."

"That's the problem. It's so easy for you to say that."

"Nick—"

I didn't hear whatever he was going to say because I was walking away. I walked out of the courtroom, took the stairs down to the first floor—I didn't want to get caught in an elevator with the Agnotti family—and was about to leave the courthouse when my beeper went off again. I took a quick look at it. It was the same 864 number that had beeped me a half an hour ago. It had to be someone I knew. Curiosity got the better of me and instead of leaving the courthouse I cut back to the payphones.

The call rang once and was picked up.

"Is this Nick," the voice asked.

I said it was before I recognized the voice. "Nello?"

"Yes. I'm at Cook County Hospital. Is there any possibility you can come here?" He must have been standing near a payphone, which explained why he beeped me twice in quick succession.

"Are you hurt? What happened?"

"I'm fine. Something happened to Tyrone, though. He has an infection. They won't tell me more than that. And he won't see me. Can you come?"

"I don't know what you think I can do."

"I don't know, maybe they'll tell you what's wrong with him."

They wouldn't. And I certainly couldn't lie and say I was Tyrone's family. And I was pretty sure doctors only talked to family members. Still, I found myself agreeing to go. County Hospital was on my way home.

"I can only be there for a few minutes."

"That's fine. Thank you, thank you."

Cook County Hospital was about eight stories tall and half a mile wide. Its architectural style was best described as early wedding cake. If there was an embellishment to be had, they'd stuck it on. The façade had columns, cherubs, ribbons and bows, lions, goats and what looked to be fig leaves without genitalia to hide. The predominant colors were beige, yellow and grime.

A cab dropped me off at the front entrance with its unembellished, blue metal awning that had been grafted onto the building sometime in the sixties, seemingly by an architect who'd never been shown the rest of the building. Nello had suggested I meet him in a waiting room on the fourth floor, so I went directly to an elevator without dawdling. The place was crowded, the elevator small and there was a smell in the air I could only describe as fear.

I found Nello standing in the hallway on the fourth floor near the elevator. He wore a colorful crewneck sweater and a pair of jeans. He looked tired. Almost as tired as I felt. "When did he come in?"

"Yesterday."

"How did you find out he was here?"

"My friend, Evan, he heard about it. Called me."

"You said he has an infection. That's all you know?"

"Yeah, that's all I know."

I remembered that he had the stomach flu when I saw him. Maybe he hadn't had that. Maybe he was working his way up to appendicitis or something. Of course, that had nothing to do with why I'd become involved with Nello Mosby. I wondered for a moment if I should tell him what I thought happened to him while I was there. But then I took a good look at our surroundings; outdated, barely clean, in need of paint. I couldn't tell him there. It was too awful.

"Where is he?" I asked.

"He's in 410. Second room down on the right. He starts yelling every time I try to go in. I had to beg them not to throw me out of the hospital entirely."

"Okay," I gave him a nod and walked a short way down the hall to room 410. It was a decent sized room, but there were ten beds; four on each side of the room and two floating in the middle. There was an elaborate system of curtains hanging from the ceiling to give the illusion of privacy. Tyrone Carter was in the first bed to the right as I walked in. He was hooked up to an IV and didn't look so good. It wasn't warm, but he'd pulled his hospital gown down so he was topless. I could see a bit of bandage on the left side of his belly.

"What are you doing here?" he asked.

"Nice to see you, too. Nello called me."

"Can you make him go away?"

"Probably. I'll need some information first."

"No. Just make him go away."

"When I saw you before you said you had the stomach flu. That was a lie."

"I didn't say I had the stomach flu, I said I had a stomach thing."

"Okay, my mistake." Then I remembered Evan Parker saying someone got 'scratched' at Jay-Jay's. "You got knifed in the stomach. Didn't you? Who knifed you?"

He looked at me suspiciously. "It's just an infection."

"Yeah. It's just an infection. That's why the hospital called the police." I didn't know that, but it was protocol if a patient had clearly experienced violence. One good lie deserved another, so I said, "I used to be a police officer. I can find out what happened to you."

"Stabbed. With a bottle. Okay?"

"About ten days ago? On the Friday night Nello can't remember?"

Reluctantly he nodded. Someone moaned on the other side of the curtain reminding me that we weren't alone. There was no chair in Tyrone's tiny space, so I sat on the bed and leaned in close.

"The blood on Nello's clothes, that was yours. Underneath the blood was semen. A *lot* of semen. Was any of it yours?"

"No. It wasn't." He was angry when he said it.

"What did you tell the police happened to you?"

"That I got mugged. That when I told this guy I wouldn't give him any money he picked up a broken bottle and stabbed me."

"You got stabbed with a broken bottle inside one of the private rooms at Jay-Jay. Do you want to tell me what happened or should I keep guessing?"

He took a moment and then decided to tell me. "I got to Jay-Jay's late. I'd been drinking at home, upset that Nello dumped me like yesterday's garbage. I hadn't been at the bar too long when someone said a drunk guy was giving blow jobs in one of the private rooms. I thought,

Why the fuck not? You know? So I go back to the room and the drunk guy is Nello. He was out of it. He didn't know what was going on. He was practically asleep. My so-called friend Jellyroll takes out his dick because it's his turn and I just, I kind of flipped out. I broke a bottle and threatened him. It turned into a fight and Maurice-Maurice got the bottle away from me and stabbed me. I don't think he meant to, though, he just did. It worked though. After that, they left Nello alone. I carried him out of there. Walked him home. Put him to bed."

"You were bleeding the whole time."

"It bled a lot at first but then it slowed down. I thought it was going to be okay, you know?"

"You need to tell Nello what happened."

"I can't. He'll hate me."

"No, he won't. You saved him. He deserves to know you're a hero."

"Those guys. They were my friends. They thought they were doing me a favor. Making him pay... That I wouldn't care."

"They were wrong. Look, if you don't tell Nello, then I have to."

"Why? Why do you have to?"

"Because that's what he paid me to do. Do you love him?"

"Yeah."

"Then you should be the one to tell him. It's the only chance you have to get him back."

He sat with that for a moment. I could see his mind working. The thing was, he had nothing to lose and everything to gain. He must have figured that out. Because he finally said, "Send him in."

Chapter Twenty

There were several cabs sitting in front of the hospital. I got into the first one, a dilapidated Ford from Speedy Cab and gave the driver my address. I sat back and closed my eyes. I didn't care what route he took—there weren't any good ones—and I didn't care how long it took. I felt marginally better. Maybe I'd done something good; I wasn't sure. It wasn't enough to make up for the last few days, though. I wasn't sure what would be.

A kid I knew when I was in fourth grade had a tumbler that polished stones. We'd watch it turn and turn and turn and then take out stones and marvel at how smooth they were, how pretty they were. I felt like I was doing that with Jimmy's case. A bar owner made a complaint. A crooked cop investigated it with his fists. Mickey, the beaten-up bagman, went to Jimmy and confessed his confession. And then Jimmy plotted to bring down the investigation. Or Jimmy *and* his granddaughter. Why? Why did it all happen?

I fell asleep in the back of the cab. The driver had to wake me up and tell me to go inside my building when we got there. As I walked up to the entrance I reached into my pants pocket looking for the Swatch to check the time. I didn't have it anymore. The Swatch was gone. I'd thrown my jacket away—along with my jeans and shirt—and the Swatch was still in the pocket. I didn't know what time it was. Somewhere around two o'clock maybe?

I walked into the apartment and found Ross watching *All My Children*. I stood there for a moment. Numb.

"Have they said anything more about the shooting?" I asked. "Is Mickey still alive?"

"Critical condition."

Okay. Not great, but alive.

"Where did you get those clothes?" Ross asked. "They're so…not you."

I didn't answer him.

"Where's Joseph?"

"He went to work."

I was glad he felt good enough to go to work, but I missed him being there. I nodded at Ross and then went into the bedroom and fell onto the bed. Within seconds I was fast asleep.

I dreamed I was being chased up a long staircase that didn't go anywhere, that suddenly dead-ended at a ceiling, which meant that whoever was chasing me was about to catch me, and just so I wouldn't get caught I woke up. I was sweaty and thick. I was also hungrier than I've ever been. My guess was I'd fallen asleep around one. At some point, half-asleep, I must have taken off the clothes that Mrs. Barnes had bought me since I was just wearing a pair of baby blue boxers. Looking out my window at the lake, it was darker but still light. The sun going down somewhere behind us had turned the sky pink.

I guessed it was around six. Joseph should be home soon. We could go somewhere and have dinner. Practically crawling out of bed, I was still desperately tired, I walked out into the living room. Ross gave me a concerned look.

"There you are. We were worried."

"We? Did Joseph come home already?"

"Oh my God. Nick. You've been asleep for twenty-six hours."

"What?"

"Last night, we tried to wake you up but you were out cold."

I had the vaguest memory of Joseph's voice, of Joseph cuddling me. I'd thought it was a dream. A lovely dream. But no, he wasn't, he didn't…

"You're teasing me. I've only been asleep for a couple hours."

He picked up the newspaper sitting next to him. "October 30th."

Taking the newspaper, I scanned the front cover. There was a big story about Jimmy's trial. Someone had the bright idea to give a baby a baboon heart. People were starving in Africa. But nothing about Mickey, which meant he must be still alive. It was definitely not Monday's news. Shit, I'd slept away a whole day.

"I'm starving. When does Joseph get home?"

"Not until late. He's with the altar boys tonight."

"The what?"

"That's what I call them. It's a support group for ex-priests."

This was news to me. "How long has he been doing that?"

"A while. They usually meet on Fridays."

"Oh."

So that was why I didn't know about it. We didn't talk about our Friday thing. Right away I wondered what that meant. Did it mean he wasn't fooling around much and was just going to this ex-priest thing? Or did it mean he went to an ex-priest orgy every week?

"Some guy came by and left this," Ross said, nodding at a paper bag sitting next to him on the couch. "It's a bag full of money. I had to look. I mean…it could have been a bomb."

"It's all right. I don't care. Did you count it?"

"A little. It's around ten thousand."

The money was obviously from Jimmy. No one else in the world would give me ten grand in cash. And it wasn't the first time he'd sent by a bag of money. But it would be the last. Right then, I decided to drive out to Oak Park and give it back to him. I didn't want his money. I didn't like what taking money from Jimmy did to my life.

"I'm going to take a shower," I told Ross. "Is there anything to eat?"

"Leftover pizza. Do you want me to heat it up?"

"No. I like it cold."

"Are you okay, Nick?"

"I will be."

Twenty minutes later, I was clean, my stomach was full, and I was on my way to Oak Park. Oak Park is a small, attractive little town just west of Chicago. I think it had a couple of famous Frank Lloyd Wright buildings scattered here and there. The average income could best be described as "fat cat" and has been for a long time. I was always surprised when I didn't get stopped at the border. Though I imagine having ten grand on the front seat next to me would have gotten me a pass.

Jimmy's house was a two-story, brick colonial. Just as I'd come to expect, there was a brand new, black 1985 Cadillac Sedan Deville sitting in the driveway. Caddys had gotten dull. I guess you could say they were elegant, understated, classic even; they were also pretty indistinguishable from a Chevy Impala. A little too understated for the price, if you asked me.

I parked across the street. I grabbed the bag and walked up to Jimmy's house. The temperature was somewhere in the mid-forties. The thin jean jacket I wore wasn't doing much to keep me warm. I knew if I was smart I'd keep the money and buy myself a whole new wardrobe. I didn't have any plans to be smart. I rang Jimmy's bell and about a minute later Rose Hansen answered the door. She wore tailored slacks and a colorful scarf around her neck. There was something different about her right off.

"Is it the maid's night off?" I asked.

"What do you want, Mr. Nowak? The trial is over."

"I'd like to talk to Jimmy."

"Did he send for you?"

I realized then she must have known much more than she'd pretended to. She certainly understood that people didn't drop in on her father uninvited.

"Would you ask Jimmy if he'll see me?"

I could tell she wanted to say no, but wasn't sure she should. Then something seemed to click and she said, "Why don't you follow me."

Rose led me through the well-appointed house to the kitchen, then down the stairs into the basement. I'd been there before. Jimmy's hobby was mixology. He'd had a full bar built in his cellar, complete with varnished wood paneling, red leather stools, and a glossy black marble bar. When we got to the bottom of the stairs, I saw that a table had been set up for cards. Deanna and Turi sat opposite each other. Beverly Harland sat between them, red-faced and blurry. Apparently, she'd fallen off the wagon. I'd have to remember to tell Sugar Pilsen; she'd get a kick out of that.

Jimmy was behind the bar in a white shirt and suspenders. He looked bent and frail. I wasn't sure whether it was time or the trial that had beaten him down, but something had. Rose started to take a seat at the card table, they must have been playing bridge or euchre or some other game for partners. Rose expected that they'd pick up their game where they'd left off, presumably because Jimmy was about to throw me out.

To her surprise, Jimmy said, "Give Nick and me a few minutes."

The card players got up and went upstairs. Beverly nearly stumbling on the way up. When Jimmy and I were alone, I sat down at the bar, putting the bag of cash next to me. Jimmy glanced at the bag, then without asking poured me a Johnnie Walker Red on the rocks. I didn't touch it.

"What was the trial about, Jimmy? It didn't have to happen. Babcock and his crew could have postponed the whole thing until you turned a hundred." Or died, which was what I really meant.

With a shaky hand, he poured himself a bit of Cointreau in a tiny fluted glass. He sipped it. "Family. It was about family."

"I don't understand."

"No, I don't expect your sort would."

I was tempted to fling my drink in his face. "Your sort," I knew what he meant by that. Unfortunately, I wanted to know why everything had happened the way it had. So he stayed dry.

"Explain it to me, Jimmy. How was that about family?"

"You're right, Babcock could have kept me out of prison. But that was never important. I would have gone to prison. I wouldn't have minded. But there was more at stake. The money."

"What do you mean, the money?"

"If they'd convicted me they would have taken the money, my business, the casino, the bank accounts, all of it. They take everything you have. I did this for my family. I did this for my Rosa. For Dina."

"For money. You did this for money."

"For my family."

"People died. Christian died. Christian's friend died. A valet who worked for you died. Three innocent people. And Mickey, Mickey almost died. All so that your daughter and your granddaughter can keep their allowances?"

I saw a spark in his eye. I'd pissed him off. Well, good. Let him be pissed off.

"I told you…your sort wouldn't understand."

"I understand just fine. It's your sort that doesn't get it."

And then I walked out, leaving ten thousand dollars on the bar.

###

St. Tony's was my second hospital in two days. It was smaller than Cook County, cleaner, quieter and probably safer. Even the architecture was better. Six stories, two colors of brick—both red—a couple of different architectural styles that showed it had been added on to, but styles that somehow managed to belong together.

Stopping briefly at a visitor's desk, I found out Michelangelo Troccoli was on the third floor in room 307. I took a narrow elevator up to the floor and then made my way down the hall to Mickey's room. The room was small and had only two beds, with a curtain separating them. The bed near the door was empty. Mickey was by the window. The bed was raised so he was sitting up. He was still on an IV, but he didn't look too bad. Next to the bed was a young boy in an over-large red flannel shirt and ripped jeans. It took a moment before I realized it wasn't a young boy. It was Gary Glenn in boy drag.

"Hey Mickey, how are you feeling?" I asked.

"I'm going to be fine. Yeah."

"Good, glad to hear it."

"I hear Jimmy got off. That's good, isn't it?"

"If you're Jimmy." It might have been better for Mickey if he'd have gotten to testify about Devlin nearly beating him to death. Or maybe it didn't matter. I assumed Jimmy would make sure no one hurt him. At least, I hoped so.

Gary Glenn stood up and said, "I'm going to get a coffee. I'll let you boys talk."

As soon as Gary Glenn walked around the curtain, a smile burst across Mickey's face. "She came back."

"I guess she did," I said. I had no idea if that was a good thing or a bad thing. I changed the subject with, "How long do you think you'll be in here?"

"Couple weeks, they said. Then I have to go to this rehab place."

"Oh, I see…" That sounded like he was hurt worse than he'd said.

"I can't feel my belly button right now."

That wasn't good. I kept it light by saying, "Belly buttons are over-rated."

"Yeah, but I can't feel my dick either."

Dicks were not over-rated.

"I'm sorry Mickey."

"What are you sorry for? It's just temporary. I'm gonna be just fine."

"That's good to hear."

"That's why I'm going to rehab. To get everything working again."

"That makes sense." It didn't. He was going to rehab to learn how to get through life without his legs. And without his dick.

"Doctors don't always know what they're talking about. You wait and see."

"I still want to apologize, Mickey."

"Why? You didn't do anything wrong?"

"I was supposed to protect you. You got hurt."

He shrugged. "It doesn't matter. I'm happy as a pig in shit. I mean it. Jimmy's paying for all this, I'm never going to have to worry about nothing, my girl came back to me, and the drugs in here, man they're good."

"Well, I'm glad you've got such a positive attitude. Keep that up. It'll help a lot."

I had to get out of there. I could think of about a hundred reasons he shouldn't have a positive attitude and I didn't want any of them coming out of my mouth.

"Listen, Mickey, my boyfriend's waiting for me, so I've gotta go. You take care. And if you need anything you just call me."

I gave him a little wave goodbye—we'd fucked a few times, but that didn't make us huggers—and then I walked out of the room. In the hallway, I ran into Gary Glenn and almost knocked the cup of coffee out of her hands.

"So you're back with Mickey?"

"Of course, I'm back with Mickey. How could I resist the melodrama? I'm a real life Lana Turner starring in her very own Douglas Sirk Technicolor marvel."

I knew who Lana Turner was but the rest was gobbledygook. It all sounded pretty cynical, that much I could figure out. And it was probably meant to hide the way she was really feeling. Just like the flannel shirt was meant to hide her Beverly Hills boob job.

"I guess you meant it when you said you loved him."

"Why wouldn't I?"

"He doesn't seem like a real convenient kind of person to love."

"Yeah, well… neither am I, darling."

Chapter Twenty-One

Joseph walked into the apartment around eleven. Ross and I were watching David Brenner guest host *The Tonight Show*. He was making silly with Suzanne Somers. She was all right, but Ross was really excited about someone named Elvira who they'd announced as a guest on Halloween night. I wasn't sure who she was and Ross' telling me she was a modern day Morticia Addams didn't help any.

I was sitting in one of the director chairs when Joseph came in and kissed me on the head. I reached up and grabbed him by the back of the neck and pulled him into a real kiss. It was a kiss like quenching a thirst, though it just left me thirsty for more when Joseph pulled away.

"Now, now, dear, the children are still awake," he said.

Ross immediately let his head fall onto his chest and began to fake snore. Joseph ignored him and got into the other director's chair.

"What's this I hear about a costume you got me?" I asked Joseph. There was something wonderful about the question. No one died because he bought me a costume. No one got beaten. No one got stabbed. The worst that would happen would be that I'd get embarrassed wearing it. And that was wonderful.

"Should I show it to him?" Joseph asked Ross.

"Yes. He'll wear it."

Joseph got up and went to the closet by the front door.

"It better not be a G-string," I said as he went.

"It's not."

A moment later he was holding a trench coat in one hand and a hat in the other. At first, I only saw the coat. "Holy shit, I need that." It was perfect. It would hide my gun easily. It was warm enough. A decent sweater underneath and I could wear it most of the winter. If I put on a pair of slacks I could wander around the Loop all day and no one would think twice. It was just what I needed.

While I was thinking about all that, I'd grabbed the coat away from Joseph and put it on. It fit perfectly. I was checking out the pockets. I loved pockets. And I needed them for my beeper, the remote to my phone machine, extra bullets, spare change, CTA tokens, my little black address book, the small notebook I liked to carry around, an extra condom or two in case it was Friday—

"Nick, it's a joke. Not a Christmas gift."

"What?"

Joseph held out the hat, a brown fedora with a black band. "Oh. I get it." I put the hat on and said, "Ha-ha, I'm a private eye."

"Isn't that the perfect costume for you?" Joseph asked.

Except that I was a private eye, so it wasn't really a costume. I didn't say that though, for fear that he'd put me in a pair of brown underpants and call me Tarzan.

"It's the perfect costume," Joseph repeated.

"What are you wearing?"

"My dog collar."

"You're going as a priest. These aren't very original costumes."

"I'm wearing my dog collar and a black Speedo. I'm going as a slutty priest."

Okay, I probably deserved that. I'd once called him a slutty priest when I was mad at him. "Are you serious? I'm just a plain ordinary private eye and you're a slutty priest."

"I didn't say you had to wear anything under the trench coat. You can be a slutty private eye, I'm okay with that."

Just the idea of my slutty priest made me say, "I think we have to go to bed now. Good night, Ross."

"What if I'm not sleepy?" Joseph asked.

"Good, I don't want you sleepy."

I started pushing him toward the bedroom. "Good night, Ross. Put in your earplugs."

"Not on your fucking life," Ross yelled as I was closing the door. I pushed Joseph up against the door and kissed him. I pressed up against him wanting to touch as much of him as possible. I reached out and flicked the overhead light off, leaving the room lit by just moonlight. I stopped kissing him but kept my lips nearly on his.

"So what's this I hear about altar boys?"

"That's Ross' joke. It's just a group of former priests sitting around wondering what we're going to do with our lives now." He brushed his lips against mine, teasing me.

"They must hate you."

"Why? Why would they hate me?"

"Because now you're going to live happily ever after."

I unbuckled his belt, unzipped his khakis and pushed them down, then I grabbed his prick though his black bikini briefs.

"Speaking of living happily ever after, I made an appointment with a therapist."

"Oh. Well, that's good." I thought it was terrible. If someone was going to change Joseph I wanted it to be me.

"It is good."

"If it's what you want to be, I guess you should know what it's like…on the couch."

"Yeah, I should know what it's like on the couch."

I didn't like the subject, so I changed it by pulling his silky, hard cock out of his briefs. I got on my knees and before I took him into my mouth, I said, "I've missed you. I feel like I've been trying to get back to you for days."

"I missed you, too. Ah—"

With his dick deep in my throat, I took his balls into one hand and gently squeezed. I let my middle finger creep behind them, rubbing, exploring, until I got it over his hole. Then I pressed. He moaned. I circled my target and then pushed. It was dry but my finger still went in.

My head bobbed up and down, as my finger searched for just the right spot. My free hand explored his belly, which was expanding in and out with his breathing. He grabbed my head, fingers in my hair. His hips pumping.

"I'm gonna cum," he gasped, trying to pull his cock out of my mouth. Pulling my finger out of his ass, I grabbed both hips and wouldn't let go. He shivered and I felt the cum rise through his shaft and hit the back of my throat.

"Oh shit."

I held onto him until he was done.

"Nick, you're not supposed to—"

I finally released him.

"I'm not worried. Shut up." It was hardly the first time I'd swallowed his cum.

I stood up and pulled him over to the bed. I unbuttoned his shirt while he kicked off his shoes and stepped out of his pants and underwear. Once he was naked, I pushed him onto the bed. Peeling off my own clothes, I took in the beauty of him. In the moonlight he seemed to shimmer, his skin so pale. And he was smiling at me, showing me his broken tooth, the slight imperfection that made him so real, so vulnerable.

Lifting both his legs into the air, I opened him up, putting my tongue where my finger had been. Circling, teasing, finally darting in and pushing. After a bit, I slipped a finger back in; easier now that it was wet. He was beginning to wiggle, beginning to want. I slipped a second finger in.

"Oh God…Nick, I want you, want you inside me."

I ignored him. Took my fingers out of him and went back to teasing him with my tongue. I listened to his breathing, listened to it quicken to a pant. Then I sat up, reached over to the orange crate and opened the little wooden box where we kept the condoms and lube. While I was getting ready, Joseph turned over and said, "Do it doggie style."

"No, I want to see you," I said.

"It's dark in here."

"It's light enough."

I had the condom on by then so I flipped him over and put some KY on his hole, spreading it around. Lifting his ankles, I pushed into him, our eyes locked. I started fucking him, slowly, easily, rocking, until he whispered, "Stop being nice."

Picking up speed, pounding into him, driving us across the bed until we were bracing ourselves with lube-y hands on the wall behind the bed. Ruining my paint job, but I didn't care. Couldn't care. Because there he was, tucked beneath me, my dick inside of him, joy and awe on his face, glistening pre-cum on his belly.

"I can't wait any longer," I said.

"Go ahead, come for me."

And then I did, in one sweet, agonizing burst after another all the while staring into my lover's eyes. I caught my break and was about to pull out. But Joseph said, "No, stay there." He held me inside of him and jacked off. It didn't take long and he was coming on his belly. And still, he didn't want me to pull out.

"Stay."

My erection was fading but I stayed inside him. Bent over him and kissed him. Pressed our sweaty, cum-covered bodies together. And I thought, *family*. This is my family, my love, my heart. Joseph. And Ross. And Brian. And Terry. And Harker. And Daniel. They were all my family. Jimmy English didn't think 'my sort' would understand. Fuck him. Fuck Jimmy English.

When Joseph finally let me pull out, I grabbed the condom at the base so it didn't slip off. As soon as I was out all the way, I knew something wasn't right. I got out bed quickly, went to the door and turned on the overhead light. Its harsh, blaring glare stripped away the moonlight. I looked into my hand and saw that the condom had split and fallen through. There wasn't any cum in the reserve tip. I didn't see cum anywhere. I'd come inside Joseph. The condom had broken and I'd come inside him.

The hair on the back of my neck stood up, my heart picked up speed, my stomach clenched. I looked at Joseph and said, "The condom broke."

He looked at me, somewhat blandly and said, "Oh. I guess that happens."

I couldn't say anything. I had no idea how he could be that calm. He knew my history. He knew about Harker. He knew I'd been with Ross while he was with Earl. I'd been with both of them after they'd gotten infected.

"Nick, you're healthy. I'm healthy. There's probably

nothing to worry about."

"You know there's a lot to worry about."

"No, that's the point. We don't *know* anything."

"But…Harker…Ross…"

"We don't know." He frowned at me. "Throw that thing away and come back to bed."

Quietly, I opened the bedroom door and in the dim light walked around the corner to the bathroom, threw the condom into the toilet and flushed. Then I went back into the bedroom and got into bed. Joseph slipped an arm around me and pulled me close.

"Go to sleep," he whispered.

I tried, I wanted to, but the only clear thought I had, a thought that grabbed me and would not let go was, "What had I done?"

ALSO BY MARSHALL THORNTON

Desert Run

Full Release

*The Perils of Praline, or the Amorous Adventures of a
Southern Gentleman in Hollywood*

*Praline Goes to Washington, or the Erotic Misdeeds of a
Newly Native Californian in Our Nation's Capitol*

The Ghost Slept Over

My Favorite Uncle

Femme

IN THE BOYSTOWN MYSTERIES SERIES

Little Boy Dead

Boystown: Three Nick Nowak Mysteries

Boystown 2: Three More Nick Nowak Mysteries

Boystown 3: Two Nick Nowak Novellas

Boystown 4: A Time for Secrets

Boystown 5: Murder Book

Boystown 6: From the Ashes

Boystown 7: Bloodlines

Boystown 8: The Lies That Bind

Lambda Award-winning author Marshall Thornton is known for the best-selling *Boystown* mystery series. Other novels include the erotic comedy *The Perils of Praline, or the Amorous Adventures of a Southern Gentleman in Hollywood*, *Desert Run* and *Femme*. Marshall has an MFA in screenwriting from UCLA, where he received the Carl David Memorial Fellowship and was recognized in the Samuel Goldwyn Writing awards. He is a member of Mystery Writers of America.